N
AT   SIGHT

A LOVE STORY BY..

CJ HOWARD

Summary

Haley had nothing to lose but everything to gain.

A new reality TV show was launching and the prize was a cool $100,000.

She would be married to a complete stranger and their lives would be followed for the next year. If they make it to the end they both get paid, if they divorce they lose everything.

The man she is to marry is sales executive Ethan Richards and the two of them must learn to get to know each other, to work together and get on together all with the cameras following their every move. Something that is not going to be easy with a scheming production crew determined to cause mayhem to boost ratings.

And when sparks really do begin to fly between the two of them, the question has to be asked, is this for love or is this for money?

Copyright Notice

Contents

Chapter 1

The warm southern California sun glinted off the sea and the buildings in downtown Los Angeles. It drew heat in undulating invisible streams from the black streets and dew to the skin of people walking around in it. It shone brightly off the cars that stopped and went, and stopped again along the highways and roads in the widespread city.

There was one car that reflected the sun's brilliance off its shiny black paint, until the car ducked beneath the sheltering cover of the driveway of one of the skyscrapers that seemed to stretch up forever.

It was surrounded by other skyscrapers, all of them reaching heavenward, as if in some race where they were all competing and then had suddenly been frozen in time, all of them partway to their destination.

The limousine driver emerged from the air-conditioned car, straightened his black cap and his black sunglasses, and then walked around the vehicle to open the passenger's side back door.

A tall athletic looking man in his later years with salt and pepper hair emerged from the car. He was immaculately dressed and wore dark sunglasses and an uninterested expression as if he had seen everything, done everything, and had no interest in seeing or doing anything more for the rest of his life.

His eyes, hidden behind his shades, were a different story entirely. They were a steel gray color; almost blue, but not quite. Not enough color to be called blue. They were sharp and cold, unfeeling and piercing, and like a black hole, they took in everything and gave nothing away.

He walked toward the building without acknowledging his driver even for a moment. The doorman opened the door and held it for him and he walked in as if there was no one around him whatsoever. Once inside, he took off his sunglasses and a secretary hurried to him and handed him a file as he looked straight ahead.

"Good morning, Mr. Wright. The meeting will be called as soon as you are ready. I'll wait for you to let me know when you're in the conference room," she told him as she kept up with his stride and let him enter the elevator alone. He turned to face her and the doors closed between them. Moments later, he was exiting onto the forty-second floor and walking toward his office. He sat at his desk and reviewed the file in his hand.

In it was a thick stack of papers that described a show he had pitched to the television networks in Los Angeles. It wasn't so much as pitched as it was sent over by courier to each one, and he received approval from three major networks and four smaller ones, each one sending back a bid on the show the same day. He had chosen one of the major networks, as their reputation was the best, their viewership was the highest, and they had outbid the other networks by more than half.

The paperwork for the upcoming reality television show was in order, so he picked up his phone and sent a text to his secretary, telling her to start the meeting in five minutes. He used the private bathroom in his office and then walked into the conference room to await the other producers of the show.

Blaine Wright had the reputation of being a cold and heartless man, one who was all business and no soul, and it was because of this reason that the other networks and producers had been stunned to see a reality show, the likes of which he had written on the documents in his folder, come from him. But he hadn't risen to become one of Hollywood's most successful executive producers by being predictable.

In less than three minutes, the rest of the producers filed into the office and as they did, Blaine's secretary stood beside the door and handed each of them a folder. They sat down and looked at Blaine expectantly and he looked back at each of them, his impenetrable gaze telling them nothing.

"The Vow," he said shortly, his eyes meeting each of theirs in turn, "is going to be aired in September. It is a reality show in which we take a man and a woman who have never met. We introduce them at their wedding to each other. They are given a small, beautiful, wedding ceremony, and then they are taken to a house that we will provide for them. They will spend nine months of the first year of marriage, which is supposed to be the hardest, living together in front of our cameras. If they make it to the end of season one, they will each receive one hundred thousand dollars."

He opened his file, and everyone else at the table opened their files as well, like an immediate echo of his action. They all looked down at the pages in front of them and he continued.

"The first order of business is that we will begin filming in two weeks. I want this cast in one week," Blaine said, as they all looked over the paperwork and several of them scribbled notes over it, made circles around certain areas, drew lines beneath some of the typed words, and seemed intently fascinated by it all.

There were eight producers sitting around the table. The one to Blaine's immediate right was a man named Murphy Newman. Murphy was balding and had a small paunch above his belt, which caused him to receive dirty looks from Blaine. Blaine had mentioned to him more than once that there was a gym facility in the office building.

Murphy always nodded and thanked him, and didn't bother to mention that it was none of Blaine's business how he looked. How he cared for his body, or cared to eat, and if he had an addiction to the French pastry store around the corner, it was, in

Murphy's opinion, no concern of Blaine's. He never said it or gave any indication that he was thinking it.

Murphy was looking carefully at the details of the show when a voice at the end of the table made his head jerk up in surprise. He stared down to the man who had dared to speak up without being asked. It wasn't that kind of meeting. Those kinds of meetings were held two floors down with people far lower on the status scale, in a room where the meeting table was littered with piles of papers and coffee cups, pens, white out, sticky notes and oftentimes broken pencils. Those meetings were held with writers, not with the Executive Producer, where no one spoke unless they were asked a question.

"Excuse me, Mr. Wright, sir," the younger man asked as he leaned forward and propped his arms on the table, twirling his pen in his fingers as he tilted his head and frowned thoughtfully.

Blaine turned his eyes to the man and gave him an icy glare. "Yes?" he asked in a clipped tone.

Murphy pursed his lips and looked back at the young man who was about to make another mistake.

"Well, sir, I was just thinking of the sanctity of marriage, you know, of actual holy matrimony. I mean, aren't we kind of cutting it a little close, having two strangers get married? Is it a real marriage? Is it just for kicks? I mean, if it's a Las Vegas wedding, then I could see a show like this maybe working and getting by, but the notes here say that the couple would be getting married here in Los Angeles, and that it is a real wedding, like with an actual officiant and everything.

"Isn't that kind of immoral? I mean, a good portion of our viewing audience at this network have a tendency to be more conservative viewers. I think if we want to play to our audience, so to speak, then we need to have a little more morality in the kind of shows we produce. I don't feel like they would want to watch a show where two strangers are suddenly put together for just less than one year to try to get a hundred grand," he said with confidence and resolution.

The room was dead silent. All of the other producers stared at him as if he was an alien. Murphy felt his heartbeat pick up to what might be considered an unhealthy pace and he was fairly sure that by the confident smile on the face of the young man sitting at the opposite end of the table, that his heart should have been beating twice as fast as Murphy's was, and he was sure that it wasn't.

Blaine didn't even blink at the young man who was opposing him. "Parker, isn't it?" he said coolly after a long uncomfortable silence.

The enthusiastic young man nodded and smiled at him. "Yes, sir. Parker Adams."

Blaine's face was still as he spoke; there was no hint of emotion or of his thoughts and what might really be going through that calculating mind of his, behind those steel gray eyes.

"Parker, perhaps you've missed it, but this is Hollywood, and in Hollywood, there is no sanctity of marriage. In fact, in most of the nation there is no sanctity of marriage. It went out of fashion in the late fifties and has never recovered.

"In fact, I'd say by the eighties that it felt a final death blow. It is uncommonly rare to find a couple who actually do marry with the intention of staying married for life, and then follow through with it all of their days.

"It may be an immoral concept of marriage, if one is looking at it that way. It is a business arrangement, like the arranged marriages that have been organized since the dawn of mankind and still continue over much of the world today. It is a dramatic gamble, and that makes it interesting to the viewing public. It makes it fascinating to watch.

"It is also a romantic endeavor, which also makes it appealing. Most of the viewing population, whether they think it is immoral or not, will watch it, hoping that it somehow works out. That, Parker, is exactly what we are counting on. It's like watching a train wreck, or a car wreck; you just can't turn away from it. You have to watch it, you are compelled to see the blood and to find out if anyone made it out of the wreckage alive.

"Throwing two complete strangers together in a marriage is going to draw the attention of the public so strongly that they will not be able to turn away. If it doesn't go well, the viewers will be fascinated with the wreckage and drama of it. If it goes well, they will be obsessed with the romance of it. This is what we call successful television, Parker."

As he spoke, Blaine's voice grew a little louder and sharper, and the rest of the producers in the room winced slightly, all of them listening and watching Blaine with a mixture of awe and fear as he spoke.

Parker shrugged and nodded. "Okay. I see where you're going with that. We may have some people who rally against it, though, so that's something to look out for." He seemed to be giving advice to Blaine, and Blaine's cheeks began to color slightly.

Murphy sank into his chair and leaned back from the table cautiously, and most of the other producers followed suit. Blaine drew a deep breath and let it out slowly and almost imperceptibly. "I am counting on that as well, Parker. You see, when there is controversy, it draws attention, and attention draws conversation and publicity, and no matter what the conversation is about, as long as there is publicity, it will bring people to their television sets and they will not be able to turn away. Controversy enables free publicity and impassioned feelings.

"We want controversy, Parker, it's a key element to success in reality shows. It's what makes people feel obligated to see it, whether they are for it or against it, because they are all hell bent on proving their point and disproving someone else's point, and in the interim, we have increased viewing numbers and substantial opportunity to charge our advertisers inflated amounts of premium to run their ads during the show! It is also one of the main reasons that shows get renewed!"

His voice was now reaching much higher volumes, and his face was turning an unpleasant shade of red. Parker seemed to finally realize that he had gone much too far and he shriveled quietly back into his seat.

"Do you have any other questions, advice, or insight for us, Parker?" Blaine asked furiously. "Or may we get on with this meeting?"

Parker shook his head quickly. "No, sir."

"Thank you! You may leave that file in front of you, go pack up your desk, and leave this building immediately. Your employment is terminated," Blaine said gruffly, recovering from his piqued temper.

Parker stared at him breathlessly and looked for a moment as if he was about to say something, when Blaine's eyes narrowed into razor thin slits and Parker seemed to think better of whatever else he was going to say. No one looked at him. He silently stood up, pushed his chair in, and left the room.

There was a thick silence in the room after the door closed. It lasted an uncomfortable amount of time, and then Blaine took a breath and looked at the men and women around him again.

"Who wants to take care of casting this?" he asked in a nearly calm tone.

One woman who was seated halfway up the table and across from Murphy nodded to Blaine. "I can do it, and I'll have Jason and Alex help me," she said in a professional voice.

The two men seated on either side of her nodded adamantly and spoke up.

"Absolutely," Jason said.

"Definitely. We can do it," Alex added, as both he and Jason looked up at Blaine with steady eyes.

Blaine smiled slightly and shook his head just a little. "The Holy Trinity," he said in a quiet voice. "Good. Get on it right away. I want it cast before the end of the week."

Alex, Valerie, and Jason were often referred to as the Holy Trinity around the office and the studios, because the three of them had figured out early that they worked together like a well-oiled machine. Whenever the three of them took on any task, it was done immediately, it was done excellently, and usually beyond the expectations of the task giver. It was like they were on a mission from God every time they took anything on, no matter the size or importance of it. When they had been given the nickname Holy Trinity, it stuck, and everyone knew them collectively. It was an earned name, and well deserved.

Murphy breathed a sigh of relief and shot Valerie a little smile. She saw it and gave him a subtle wink back. She had managed to recover the meeting and everyone in the room, aside from Blaine Wright, was grateful for it.

She flipped through the pages before her and frowned slightly. She looked up at Blaine and asked in a steady voice, "What kind of couple do you have in mind for this?"

Blaine leaned back a little and touched his finger to his chin thoughtfully. "They need to be beautiful, they need to be young, they need to be believable. They need to be attention grabbers, people that the audience will fall in love with and want to root for. People who could not only look the part of a celebrity, but also handle it well. We have no competition for this kind of a reality show, but we have competition for time slots and, of course, for viewers. Their situation must be believable, sympathetic, and engrossing."

Valerie nodded. "We will take care of it, sir. I'll have the cast bios on your desk before the end of this week."

Blaine nodded at her, then he looked down at the paperwork in front of him, and so did every other set of eyes in the room. He continued without looking up at them.

"We will send in a camera crew, not a big one, just two people if we can," Blaine continued. Murphy made notes about crew as Blaine added, "They will be filming lead-up to the wedding while the bride and groom are getting prepared; let's give them each three days of prep. This will be teaser material for the promos for the show, as well as individual interviews with the couple.

"They are to be held in seclusion with their own staff during those three days up until the wedding. I don't want them knowing anything about each other until they meet at the end of the aisle at the ceremony. After the three-day prep, we have the wedding.

"The bride may choose her colors if she wants to, but everything else is on this team. Make it a beautiful wedding that anyone would be envious of and want for themselves. Sell it," he said, looking up at them each again, and all of them nodded and scribbled on their pages.

"Murph, you're handling the wedding details," Blaine said with a glance at Murphy.

Murphy nodded. "I'm on it," he said simply and wrote endless notes on his pages.

"Now, after the wedding, the camera crew are going into the home every day from seven in the morning until ten at night, or until the couple goes to bed. We want to capture everything, shoot it all and let the editing team do their jobs and get it ready for the show the following week. I want this shot and shown quickly.

"Word travels too fast now to hold anything back longer than a couple of days. We don't shoot at night unless some sort of drama comes up, and drama at night may be written into the show later on, depending on how things go. If the couple makes it to the end of season one, then they will each receive the hundred thousand, if not, they walk away and they get nothing."

Blaine looked up from the paperwork in front of him and eyed each of them carefully. "The concept is to sell a romance to the public, an unlikely romance; two strangers meet, they fall in love over time, they overcome hardships together, and they somehow make it through to the end of the season, in love, and ready to be married for life or longer. Unless all hell breaks loose in between, we are planning, as of now, to have the romance build over the term of the season.

"The public needs to really believe it, to want them to be together, to root for them. The writers will be providing hardships for the couple along the way; cohabitation issues, trust issues, fidelity issues, and whatever else people face in their first year of marriage.

"Some of the problems will be things that several couples face, and some will be things that only a few couples face. Even in the division of sides when things get problematic, the viewers must love the couple. I do have some plans for serious issues to come up for the couple, but no one will know what those are until the week before the show where they'll be featured,"

Blaine glanced at the man sitting beside him, "not even Murphy Newman," he said with a little smile.

Murphy nodded.

"Are there any questions?" Blaine asked, looking around at all of them.

No one spoke up.

"Good. Go cast it." He closed his file, pushed his chair back and left the room. An audible collection of deep breaths was heard from everyone still sitting around the table.

Murphy looked at the Holy Trinity. "You three. I'll be dropping by the auditions, so let me know when you've got them going, please."

They looked at him and nodded, each with a genuine smile for him. He was much better liked than Blaine Wright. He handled his staff with a more empathetic hand and heart.

The three of them were still making notes, checking calendars, and murmuring softly between themselves.

Valerie Stein was of medium height, just a little shorter than Murphy. She had short dark hair that was always cut and styled so that she didn't have to do much to it. She was thin, even for Hollywood standards, and was always in a dress suit with dark heels.

On the rare, cool Los Angeles days, her skirt may be changed for dress pants, but that was about the only change she made to her daily work look. She was married to her job, and that was the way she wanted it to be. She was tough, smart, dedicated, and hardworking, and it showed in the results of everything she did.

In the so-called Holy Trinity of her, Jason Thompson, and Alex Moran, she was god. Alex and Jason respected her and listened to her, and she gave them the same courtesy, but she was the fuel behind them getting everything done. She was also the technology guru; if there were wires and a power source involved, she could work miracles in moments. There was nothing about technology, new or old, that she didn't fully comprehend and oftentimes supersede.

Jason was the same height as Valerie, though not nearly as thin. He had a stockier build, had been a high school wrestler and then traded protein drinks for beers on Monday nights for every football game he could watch. He thought in business the same way he did in sports; watch the other guy, figure out his weakness and the obvious advantage, and go for it before anyone else knows what's happening. He was a lightning fast thinker; on his feet, off the cuff, and no one could keep up with him when he got going.

The other two had learned shortly after they met him to never to play any kind of game with him that had to do with strategy, because there was no way that they could win. They had never seen him lose at chess, checkers, or even at gambling on the rare occasion that they were in a casino. It was almost as though he could figure things out so quickly that he was able to predict the future, at least up to a minute or two.

Alex Moran was a Hispanic man, undeniably handsome and unequaled in his ability to charm. If anyone could sell a glass of water to a drowning man, it was Alex. He had long, wavy black hair, dark brown eyes and a dimpled smile that got him anywhere he wanted to go.

It didn't hurt that he also spoke seven languages fluently and knew how to dance practically every dance that came up, and had graduated in the top two percent of his university class with a Master's in business and communication. He knew the ins and outs of any kind of business deal or legality that could possibly come up. Studying law was a hobby of his, and while he had no interest in working in law, he was profoundly useful with his intimate knowledge of it.

Murphy rose up from his chair and looked at Jason. "Make sure that Parker made it out okay," he said quietly. Jason nodded and Murphy headed for the door. "Thank you," he said as he walked out.

There was nothing he could do to save Parker's job, but he didn't want any problems coming back up before the man walked out of the building for the last time. He walked to his office and sat down in his chair, opening up the file once more to look it over with some peace and quiet around him, so that he could think about how to make this new show work best, and how to make everyone in the country want nothing more than to watch The Vow.

*

Not too far away in distance, but about a billion miles away in lifestyles from Wright, Murphy, and the Holy Trinity, sat two young women. It had been three days since the meeting in the skyscraper, and at that moment, that fact was completely irrelevant to both of them as they looked at their menus and tried to decide what to get for lunch at the little cafe that sat facing the golden, sunny beach of the Pacific Ocean.

The server came by their table and the shorter and rounder of the two women looked up and smiled. "I'll have the cheeseburger meal. Spicy fries, and please change my coke to a strawberry shake."

Her best friend looked at her and grinned, shaking her head. Then she looked up at the waiter. "I think I'll have a Caesar salad and an iced tea, thanks," she told him, and he disappeared.

"Leslie, I don't know how you can eat like that. You are the single most un-California beach girl I ever knew, but I gotta tell you, I love you for it." Haley grinned at her and gave her a wink.

Leslie was round and curvy, but she held it so well, and she was so confident, that it didn't look bad on her at all. She maintained a sexiness and brightness about her that women of every size and shape envied, and men hungered for. Leslie was never without two or three men after her at any given time, and she enjoyed them, but none of them had managed to steal her heart away.

She looked at Haley and laughed. "I'm happy; I love the way I look and I am living my life the way I want to. What if I kick off this afternoon in traffic on I-5? I'm gonna die happy. That's what's going to happen. I'm not going to die with a carrot stick and a sliver of celery in my belly, wishing I had gone ahead and ordered salad dressing with it."

Haley laughed, and it was light and silvery, like bells that made the listener look up to find, and hope to hear again. It was an infectious laugh, and it made Leslie laugh back at her.

"Well, I'm going to look for more work, so I want to be a little mindful of what I'm putting into my body this week. I'm not driving on I-5 today, or anytime soon, so I plan on being alive for a while, and I have some serious competition for employment out in this city." She gave a slight frown and rolled her eyes.

Leslie sighed with disappointment. "I know. Everyone's looking for work. I would see about getting you on at my office, but they aren't hiring for anything decent, and you don't know much about international shipping."

Haley shook her head as she looked at her friend. She was extraordinarily beautiful, with light wide-set almond shaped eyes, almost a sea green color, framed by thick long dark eyelashes. Her cheeks were high and arced, giving her an exotic look; as if she had somehow been the product of several different heritages put all together in one person, and the best traits of each had come out in her. Her skin was the color of chocolate with just a touch of cream, her hair was naturally curly, but the curls were big and soft, hanging down to the middle of her back.

She had a long, graceful neck, a strong jaw line, and full, shapely lips that were oftentimes curved into a smile. Her nose was rounded and curved gently at the end, with no sharpness about it. People often said that it was cute, but the rest of her was often complimented as being elegant. She stood out in a crowd, there was no denying that.

She crossed her long shapely legs and leaned back in her seat, her fit and very feminine form relaxing gently as she looked at Leslie.

"Thanks, I appreciate the thought. I don't think I could work where you are. It's not really my cup of tea. I just can't keep working at the office where I am now. I love the realtor I work for, but I don't like the woman I work with, and I am not thrilled with the work that I do every day. It's not fulfilling. It's not what I want to do with the rest of my life, or even the rest of my year, if I'm being honest," she said with a sigh.

The server brought their drinks and smiled at her. "These are complimentary," he said, giving her a grin and a nod.

Leslie giggled at her. "Thanks honey! I love going places with you. You always get spoiled."

Haley rolled her eyes and giggled a little. "No, I don't always get spoiled."

Leslie raised one eyebrow and gave her a look that clearly stated she didn't believe her one bit.

"So. What do you want to go do for a job?" she asked Haley, poking at her strawberry shake with her straw.

Haley frowned a little. "I have no idea. I wish I was able to sell my art and make enough to live off of it. I've attempted to get it into as many coffee shops and galleries as I can, but there just doesn't seem to be a market for it, and I don't have time to make enough to replace the art I sell in a timely enough manner that I could make a living at it."

"What about working in a gallery?" Leslie suggested hopefully.

Haley shook her head. "I've tried. They want you to babysit the galleries without actually paying you to be there, and then they give you five feet of wall space in the back of the place to show your own art. No thanks."

Leslie rubbed her chin with her hand. "There's got to be something that you could do. Let's see what I have on my daily today..." she said, pulling out her smart phone and swiping through the screens.

"You have an app for finding jobs?" Haley asked in pleasant surprise.

"There's an app for everything," Leslie told her without looking up. She skimmed through several pages and then raised her eyebrows.

"Lifeguard?" she asked, not looking up.

"No. I don't want to be out in the sun that much. This August heat has been brutal." Haley sat sipping her iced tea and looking out of the window at the city baking in near triple digits.

"Driver?" Leslie asked as she scrolled.

"No, I don't think I know the city well enough and I'd be worried about constantly having to use my GPS. Plus, I don't want to sit all day," she said with a shake of her head.

"Data analyst, sales, housekeeper, floral designer, cook, dog groomer..." she trailed off as she read along.

Haley laughed.

"Hey... this one's funny," said Leslie. "Listen to this. Network studio seeking stars for a reality show. Need a single woman and a single man to marry each other and live together for one season of the show. If successful, both stars will each receive one hundred thousand dollars. Auditions on... uh... they're tomorrow!" she said with a laugh, looking up at Haley.

"You could do it! You're single! You could marry a guy for one season of the show and then get a hundred grand. That's not even a whole year! That's nothing! You could do it! You should do it!"

Haley laughed again and shook her head. "I'd never do something like that! What would they do with someone like me?"

Leslie leaned forward and looked hard at her. "You are a gorgeous woman with a kind and beautiful heart. You would be making a small fortune in a matter of months, and while you're living with this guy, maybe you could paint and make more pieces to sell, and when you finish the show, you could get your hundred grand and open your own art gallery.

"Then you would have time to paint and make money from your art. Seriously. This is so perfect for you that it's almost like it was designed for you," she said earnestly as she reached for her friend's hand. "Haley, you have to do this. It's perfect!" she continued.

Haley sighed and looked at her friend in slight consternation. "I'm not the kind of girl that anyone chooses for a thing like that. I wouldn't make it."

Leslie raised her eyebrows. "You're never going to know if you don't try. You know who Wayne Gretzky was? He was a hockey player in Canada. He said you miss one hundred percent of the shots you don't take. This is a gamble, sure, but so is everything else. You go to this audition, you try out for it, you leave and focus on finding another job. If they never call you, you're already out there looking for something else.

"If they do call you, then you are all set. It's not going to hurt anything. I really feel like you should try this.

I think you'd be making a mistake not to at least go to the audition."

She sat back and looked at Haley resolutely.

Haley was thoughtful and still for a moment as she let the thought roll around in the back of her head. Then the humor of the whole thing struck her and she laughed at Leslie and sighed.

"You're serious about this!" she chuckled in wonder.

Leslie nodded and looked at her with wide eyes. "I'm dead serious. I'll drive you myself. I can just imagine you getting it and having time to do your art! It would be so perfect."

"It would be bizarre! How could I marry someone I don't know?" she asked as she knitted her brows just thinking of it.

Leslie shrugged. "Who says you have to do anything with him other than just be married to him? The least you could do is just go check it out; I mean, if you get there and you don't like the deal, then leave. You could get there and find out that this is the best thing you could ever do. I just want you to have a chance at it. Think of it! A hundred grand! Your own gallery! I can't stand it! You have to do it. I'm not letting you out of it."

Just like that, Leslie put her foot down and looked intently at Haley.

Haley knew she wasn't going to be able to talk her best friend out of it. "Alright. I'll go tomorrow and audition. In the meantime, what else do you have on that list of jobs?" she asked curiously.

She knew that there was less than no chance of her making it beyond the auditions, so she didn't give it another thought; she didn't want to think about it, it was the craziest idea she had ever heard of... marrying a stranger. She didn't want to listen to her friend try to talk her into it. She wanted to find a real job where she could make better money at a better place than the one where she presently was.

The waiter came with their food and delivered it with a grin at Haley, another wink, and a nod. The friends laughed a little and then ate their lunch and afterward, they went for a long walk on the beach, cooling themselves in the surf on the shoreline.

The two of them said their goodbyes and Haley didn't give the audition another thought until her alarm clock rang and she got up the next morning and walked into the bathroom and looked in the mirror. Then her eyes grew wide and she thought that even if she wasn't putting much faith into getting past any audition, she ought to at least look the part and give herself as much of a chance as she could.

She showered and did her makeup, giving special attention and accent to her eyes and lips, as she felt those were her best facial features. She pulled on a soft buttercup yellow sundress that hugged her full and inviting curves and accentuated her long legs. She slipped pearl earrings into her ears, closed a pearl necklace around her slender throat, and finished just a few moments before Leslie knocked on the door of her apartment.

"I'm coming!" she called out, grabbing her phone, keys, resume with headshot, and her purse, before pulling the door open and walking out into the bright morning sun.

Leslie took one look at her and whistled. "Gawd, woman, if it was the fifties, you'd be a pin up model for sure. Let's go!" she trilled excitedly as she gave Haley a quick hug, then turned, and hurried down the sidewalk.

An hour later, they were waiting in a long line of women who had been sectioned off from the men. There were women of every size, shape, and color, standing in the line. The details of the ad had specified twenty to twenty-five years old, and Haley had just made that cutoff at twenty-four. She suspected there would be a much longer line if the age limit hadn't been published in the ad, and she also strongly suspected that several of the women in line with her hadn't bothered to read the few guidelines posted beneath the ad, including the age limitations.

Leslie had dropped her off and, as only those auditioning were allowed to wait in line, she had said she was going to go shopping and would have her phone on her, ready to head back to pick Haley up at any time.

After two hours of waiting and moving slowly toward the front of the line, Haley finally had her turn. She entered a small room and saw three people sitting at a long table.
There were two men and one woman, who looked like she was in charge. They asked her for her resume, which she handed to them, then they asked her to read a brief script that they handed to her. She walked in front of the lights and camera that were recording, and looked into the lens, telling herself to speak to the lens as if it were her husband.

She focused and took a deep breath and read the piece, expressing emotion as genuinely as she could, and when she got to the end of it, she looked at the trio sitting at the table. They were making several notes and conferring with each other. She waited a moment, and then walked out of the lights and from the view of the camera and looked at them quietly.

Their voices were too soft to hear. The three of them looked up at her and the stockier, more rounded one looked at her carefully and asked, "You're single? You aren't currently in a relationship with anyone?"

She shook her head and smiled. "No, I am not."

He watched her for a moment and then nodded. "Okay Miss, thank you so much. You may go."

Just like that, it was over. Two hours of waiting in that long line for less than a minute with the panel at the desk. She gave their script page back to them and walked out of the door.

Haley drew a deep breath that was a sigh of relief, and she felt much lighter. She headed toward the front of the building and called Leslie.

"I'm done. It's over. I'll wait for you at the front of the building, okay?"

"How did it go?" she asked adamantly.

"I'll tell you when you get here." Haley laughed.

Fifteen minutes later, she was climbing into Leslie's car and being grilled with a hundred questions about how it went, how she felt, what she did, who she saw, how many other women were in line, what they looked like, how long it lasted, what she read, and how they responded to her.

By the time Leslie was finished with her rapid fire questioning, Haley felt as if she had gone through an entirely different audition. "Are you done?" she asked with a smile and a slightly irritated voice.

Leslie sighed and nodded. "I guess so. You know, I wouldn't have to ask you so many questions if they would just let me come in to the audition with you."

Haley nodded. "I know. I'm sorry they didn't. It would have been a lot more fun with you there!"

"It's true," Leslie raised her eyebrows and nodded at her friend. "Everything is always more fun with me around. So now what?" she asked, looking over at Haley.

"I'd like to get my mind onto something else now, like lunch and a different job. How about that?" Haley asked with a smile.

Leslie nodded and they headed off to find lunch and take another look at Leslie's job app on her phone.

Haley got a few possible job opportunities from Leslie and wrote them down to look into, and then Leslie dropped her off at her apartment and she walked in and kicked off her shoes, ready to relax. It had been a long day, and she was ready to relax.

She showered again and wrapped herself in a light robe, and then sat down with a good book to let her hair dry and get her mind off her job hunt.

She was several chapters in and mentally wrestling with herself about either putting the book down and going to make dinner, or finishing the book and ordering out for Chinese food, when her cell phone rang.

Haley picked it up and frowned at the number. She didn't recognize it at all.

"Haley Lawrence, please, said a woman's voice.

"This is Haley," she replied. "May I help you?"

"Hello, this is Valerie Stein from Kittyhawk Productions. You auditioned for a reality television series with us this morning."

Haley dropped the book and sat straight up on the sofa. "Yes..." she said quietly, her heart beginning to beat swiftly, pushing the blood through her veins and nearly drowning out the sound of the woman's voice on the phone.

"We'd like you to come in for an interview, please. Are you free tomorrow morning?"

Haley took a deep breath. An interview... that wasn't an acceptance, but it was not a rejection either. "Yes, of course. I can come in anytime tomorrow morning." She'd have to take the morning off work at the real estate office, but she knew that would be easy to do.

"Wonderful. We'll see you at ten, then," Valerie told her. "I have your email here. I'll email instructions and directions to you. Thank you for your time," she said pleasantly, and then bid her goodbye.

Haley stared at the phone in her hand, hardly able to believe the phone call that she had just had. *How it had even happened*, she wondered. It was incredible. Now she was going in for an interview. She finally let herself consider the possibility that she might actually be chosen for the show, and then she let herself really think about what that would actually mean.

She'd have to marry someone. A real wedding. A marriage to a stranger... a man she knew nothing about, and she would have to live with him for almost a whole year. Over the fall and the holidays, into the new year and the coming spring. How would she ever be able to do that? How could she promise herself to a man she didn't know for nine months, let alone any longer than that?

It was like an arranged marriage, she thought to herself. Like one of those cultures who married off their daughters to boys or men who were total strangers as nothing more than a business deal, and the family would make a profit of some kind of another.

She would be the one making the profit in this case. One hundred thousand dollars. It could be a profit and an investment in herself and her future. She had read the slightly more detailed information that the company had handed out at the audition. She could do anything she wanted after the show was over in the spring. If she wanted to divorce him, she could. It wasn't that much time. It was just one brief season. She wondered if she could really do it.

She wondered what her parents would say. Her mother was fairly liberal and open minded, but her father was quite a bit more conservative, and she knew right away that he wouldn't like it at all. He'd probably hate it, but after it was over... if she was chosen for it, and if she did it... after it was over, she could take that money and open her own art studio and gallery, and then she'd be set for a long while and she could do her art and make a living doing what she loved.

Haley gave it serious consideration and then picked up the phone and called in to her office for the next morning, letting them know that she had some personal business to attend to and would not be in until later on the following day. It was a voicemail, which she was grateful for, as she didn't have to talk with anyone about it.

She knew she would have to tell Leslie about it right away, not only for encouragement and support, but because Leslie had been far more excited about the opportunity than she had, and she wouldn't have even gone or known about it without Leslie.

Leslie's phone didn't ring a second time. Her best friend picked it up right away and asked her, "Did you hear from them? Did you?"

It was like she knew.

Haley laughed. "I did, actually. They just called."

Leslie screamed in her ear. "Oh my God, you got the part! You got the part!"

Haley tried her best to calm her friend down. "Wait, wait, wait... I don't know yet if I got the part. I am just going in for an interview. I'll probably know after that, unless I'm only part of the way through the selection process."

Leslie was quiet only a moment. "Well, that's still something! You got in! I'm so excited for you!"

Haley was quiet then and she said thoughtfully, "Leslie, have you given any thought at all to what this actually means?"

Leslie paused and then asked, "What are you talking about? What does it mean?"

"It means that if I'm chosen, I'm going to have to get married, an actual, real marriage, to a man I have never met before. I will have to stay married until the end of next spring. I haven't even met any guys I like well enough to date. What am I going to do with a husband? What if they want me to be intimate with him? What if he's a complete jerk?" she began to worry herself with the endless possibilities of everything that could go wrong.

Leslie stopped her. "Hey, now wait a minute. I'm sure that at any point, if you've had enough or you don't want things to get worse, all you have to do is walk out of the door and leave. Even if you need to get the divorce early, you'd be divorcing him anyway after the show, right?"

Haley saw her friend's logic. "Yeah, I guess you're right. I'd be getting divorced anyway."

"It's a gamble, but if you can make it to the end, think of the payoff! You could get your own studio! You wouldn't have to work anywhere else and you could focus on your art. That's why I'm pushing so much for you to do this," she said in a heartfelt way.

Haley considered it carefully. "I know you're right, I guess I'm just a little nervous... it's a huge step, but I guess I won't really worry about it, I mean, I haven't signed anything, so there's nothing to worry about until then, anyway, right?"

"Exactly right."

"If I do get in, then the biggest problem will be telling my parents." Haley laughed a little, nervous at the idea of it.

"I'm more worried about your dad than your mom, but you do have a point about them. Still, I'm really excited for you. I hope it happens."

Haley thought about it for a long moment and then smiled. "You know what? So do I. You are right. What an incredible opportunity. Even if it is weird."

 "Good luck" Leslie said with a smile that could be heard through the phone.

"Thanks, I'll let you know as soon as I find out," Haley promised.

"You better!"

Chapter2

Early morning light filtered in through the partially closed blinds, touching the walls and the floor of the decently sized bedroom, and it slowly moved up the edge of the bed, lighting the sheets and two sets of feet, before it rose up over the bodies of the two people lying there; a man and a woman.

The woman had long, wavy red hair that flared out over her back, the pillow, and the man near her. She had a slender body, a tiny waist, gently rounded hips, long legs and large enhanced breasts. Her green eyes were closed and her enhanced lips were slightly parted as she breathed in and out slowly in her sleep.

The sunlight reached her closed eyes and she awoke and rolled over, looking briefly at the man next to her. He was solidly built; muscular and strong. His skin was tanned lightly by the sun, and his long straight golden blonde hair reached to his shoulders. His hazel eyes were still closed in slumber and his long body was stretched out to the end of the bed.

The woman rubbed her eyes over her face and yawned, then pushed herself up against the pillows piled on the headboard. She reached for her phone and turned it on, sliding her finger over the screen and looking at everything that scrolled beneath her fingers.

After a few minutes, she stopped scrolling and looked intently at an ad on her phone.

She read through it twice and then her eyes grew big and her mouth opened slightly. She reached her elbow over and nudged the man sleeping beside her.

"Ethan! Ethan wake up!" she said insistently.

He mumbled and rolled over. "Mmm."

She shot him an annoyed look. "Wake up, Ethan, I want you show you this!" she frowned at him.

He opened one eye. "Mmm? What?" he asked groggily.

The woman grabbed a pillow from behind her and whacked him hard with it. "Get up! You have to see this! Now! Up, up, up!" she insisted.

Ethan raised his arms to block her attack and pushed himself upward, grabbing the pillow from her.

"Okay, okay, I'm up! What are we doing? What's going on?" He stretched and raked his hand through his long hair and then turned his head to look at her with a smile in his eyes.

"Good morning, beautiful!" he said, leaning over to kiss her cheek softly.

She batted him away and thrust her phone toward him. "Look at this!" she said excitedly.

He frowned at her dismissal of his affections and looked at her phone. "What is it?" he asked, taking it from her.

"What is it? It's only the easiest money anyone ever got. Look!" she pointed and he blinked the sleep from his eyes and then began to read.

"....reality show... auditions... marriage..." he mumbled as he skimmed over it. "I don't understand why you're showing this to me," he said with a lowered brow as he looked up at her. "Is this what I'm supposed to be looking at? This marriage show?"

She nodded quickly. "Yes! Isn't that fantastic!"

He stared at her in confusion for a moment and then a sly, flirty smile came over his lips and he slid his hand up her bare leg toward her hip. "Are you telling me you'd like to go shopping for rings? I didn't think you wanted to do anything like that. I thought you ruled that out," he said, leaning over to kiss her shoulder seductively.

She gave him a nasty look and pushed him away from her. "Stop that! I'm not giving you a hint to marry me, you idiot, I'm telling you that I want you to go audition for it!" Her eyes began to sparkle as she looked off into her distant future and he frowned again and leaned back against his own pillows.

He looked at her in utter shock. "What do you mean you want me to go audition for it? I can't do that, I'm with you! What on earth are you talking about?" He lowered both his eyebrows at her.

She sighed as if she was trying to find the patience to explain an elementary concept to a child who ought to be able to understand it but simply hadn't.

Turning toward him in annoyance, she leveled her gaze at him and spoke slowly and almost mechanically.

"I know we are together, but we won't get any money being together. This gig pays a hundred grand. Now think about that... a hundred grand... we could go anywhere and do anything we wanted to! I could go to New York and get acting lessons at the best schools and then become a big star..." She narrowed her eyes at him.

"Don't you want that for me? Isn't my happiness important to you?" She frowned and the sour look on her face gradually evolved into a serious pout as she pushed her red lips out at him and her eyes grew sad.

He watched her and felt his heart tug for her. "Oh, now Erica... please don't feel bad. I just don't think I can do this! This isn't something I would want to do, and I have no interest in it," he told her honestly.

She pouted even more. "Yes, but *I* want it, and you want me to be happy, don't you?" she asked in a little girl pouty voice.

Erica turned toward him and slowly slipped her hand along the length of his leg up to his thigh where her fingers began to squeeze and massage him as she moved herself in between his knees, looking up at him.

"It's just a teeny, tiny quick little job. It's not like I'm asking you for some huge favor. It's just a few months," she said, her eyes steady on his as she lowered her mouth to his thigh and left a long wet kiss there before she began to slink upward toward his crotch like a cat. "Just a little tiny fraction of time where you do this little bitty job, and people will love you and you'll be famous." She leaned over and kissed his other thigh, lingering there for a moment and twirling the hard tip of her tongue over his skin. He stared at her as his groin tightened and grew hard with need.

Erica gave him a sultry smile. "You'd just be doing it for show, not for real, and you'd be doing it for me, to make me happy...." She moved her mouth up to his erection and slid her tongue over the full length of it slowly, winding her way, teasing and taunting him as he groaned and let his eyes roll back in his head for a moment.

Erica wrapped her big lips around the tip of him and began to suck lightly as she traced the lines and curves of him with the edge of her tongue. She squeezed his thighs with her hands and began to suck harder on him, slipping him inch by inch into her mouth and down her throat. He groaned in desperation for her.

She moved her mouth back up and released him with a soft kiss and he opened his eyes and looked back down at her. She raised herself up, hovering over him as she spread her thighs and slid them over his groin. She arched her back and thrust her large breasts out, holding them in her hands, and then she flipped her head backward and all her long red wavy hair went sailing like a fan behind her.

Ethan reached for her and clamped his hands onto her hips, pulling her toward him breathlessly. She resisted and he gasped in need.

"I want to be happy Ethan, that's all. I don't ask for much," she said, touching herself for a moment and then reaching her hands for him. She stroked him gently at first and then more fervently as she spoke and he groaned anxiously beneath her.

"Don't you want me to be happy?" she asked with her sultry pouty face. "Don't you want to do anything you can to make me happy?"
He could barely speak. "Of... of course I do... but marriage to some strange woman..." He groaned again as she leaned toward him and caressed his bare chest with her hard nipples, her hand still moving

swiftly over his erection and making him wild with desire.

"Give me what I want then... Ethan... if you really loved me, you would do it. You would do anything I ask you, for love... If you want my love, you have to love me back, and I want you to do this for me. I want the money Ethan. I want it bad." She kissed him hard, sucking on his tongue for a moment and then looking down at him as she hovered her breasts over his face and stroked him faster, making him gasp for air and sanity.

"I do love you, Erica, but I can't..." he said in a whisper, losing himself in the heated ecstasy she was inducing in him.

"Oh, yes you can, baby, you can do anything. You just go down there today and audition for it," she said, pressing her nipple into his mouth, "you audition for it and you make sure you get it. It's just a few quick months, and then you get a divorce, you take the money, and you and I can go to New York. It's my dream, baby, don't you love me? Don't you want to help me reach my dreams?" she asked, letting go of his rock solid erection and reaching for a condom on the nightstand.

"I do want to help you..." he breathed as she lifted her breast from his mouth and sat up over his groin looking at him. He stared at her, his eyes glazed over with desperation for her, his hands canvassing her body hungrily.

She rolled the condom over him and moved above him, sliding him into her slowly as she smiled at him and leaned down toward him, gently rocking her hips against his and running her tongue up his chest to his mouth where she bit at his lips.

"Then do it for me," she said huskily to him. "Promise me, you'll go do it today." She began to move herself harder and faster over him.

He clenched his hands onto her hips and thrust himself deeply into her, feeling for certain that this must be true love. There could be no way that any woman was as incredible as Erica was, without it being true love. She began to move faster over him, stealing away his breath and all of his reasoning.

"Come on, baby, lie to them and tell them you're single, come on, do it for me... promise me..." she said in a whisper against his mouth as she rocked herself harder.

Ethan knew there was no way he could turn her down. There was nothing he wouldn't do for her. He didn't know if it was the passion burning through him, or the love in his heart for her, but he relented. "I'll go..." he gasped as she gripped him by the chest and pushed all of him into her body.

She grinned at him happily and kissed him. "Good, baby... just get me all that money. I want it bad.

Promise?" she asked as she held him tightly and moved even faster against him.

He pushed his head back into the pillows and gasped for breath. "Yes... Yes!" he cried out. "I promise!"

Moments later, he came hard, shuddering beneath her and feeling his skin shiver with a chill of release as his body was emptied and his need was sated. He caught his breath finally as she lifted herself from him and climbed off the bed, walking away from him, and all he could see was her long wild red hair, her gorgeous round ass, and her long legs as she went to the bathroom.

He sighed and covered his face with his hands, wondering what he had been thinking. He'd promised to go marry a total stranger to get a hundred thousand dollars for her. He breathed out slowly and opened his eyes, staring at the ceiling. He supposed it was what people in love did for one another.

There was the reassurance in the back of his mind that he had to actually make it through the auditions first, and if that didn't happen, he wouldn't have to marry anyone at all, and he could keep his fiery little redhead happy some other way.

She walked out of the bathroom, her body dewy and her hair wet. "Go get ready, you have to be down there pretty soon," she told him seriously. "You have to look your best. You have to win this, so you had better make yourself look hot. Move it!" she said with no amount of kindness or pleasantry.

He smiled at her and pulled himself up out of bed. It was no time at all before he was showered, shaved, and dressed to the nines in a button down shirt, a silk tie, and a matching vest and pants set. It was too hot for the jacket, so he left that off, but he rolled his sleeves up to his elbows and gave her a turn.

"Does this meet with my lady's approval?" he asked with a smile.

She eyed him critically and nodded. "Yeah, you look good. Now, go get that role, and don't forget to tell them you are single. I don't want to risk any chances of my getting that money. I'll just see you here later tonight and you can tell me how it went, okay?"

She slid a slinky blue dress on over her curves, raked a hand through her wild red hair before sliding bright red lipstick over her full lips.

He stared at her. "God, Erica, you look so good..." he said, his eyes locked on her. He moved to walk to her and kiss her, but she pushed him away.

"Don't! You'll smudge my lipstick and I just got it on. Go get that part. I want that money, baby." She gave him a seductive smile, running her hand over his crotch a few times before she winked at him and then turned and walked out of the door.

Ethan groaned and shook his head. She was a handful, there was no doubting that, and he was sure that he was in love with her. He must be, he told himself, if he was willing to marry someone else for nine months just to get enough money to take her to New York.

He made his way to the auditions, incredulous that she had found them the very morning they were happening. He got in line and waited a long while. After more than three hours in line, he walked into the little room and was handed a script to read. The moment he walked over to the panel table where the two men and the woman sat, he handed them his resume and head shot, the three of them stared at him and then looked at each other.

He was used to people doing double takes with him. He had a strong chiseled jaw and a slightly dimpled chin. His hazel eyes had flecks of gold that were brought out by all the shiny, thick, blonde hair that fell like soft gold around his broad shoulders. His physique was that of a body builder, although he didn't do too much body building. He didn't want to get too big and he wasn't interested in competitions; he just wanted to be healthy, strong, and fit, and he was definitely that.

Ethan walked over and waited for them to tell him to start. The woman hadn't taken her eyes off of him.

"Hold on one moment, please," she told him before putting her cell phone to her ear. She spoke into it briefly and then set it down.

"We need to wait for someone else to come in for your audition," she said politely.

A few minutes later, the door opened and an older man with a slight paunch, a balding head, and a bag of French pastries, came in through the door and stopped in his tracks as he eyed Ethan. He tilted his head thoughtfully and then walked over to the panel table and sat down.

"Go ahead, please," the woman told him.

Ethan lifted his head and looked into the camera, reading his lines as genuinely as he could, and when he was done, he turned and looked at the table. Every eye was on him, and then they were all talking amongst themselves.

"Do you have anything prepared that you could recite impromptu?" the man with the French pastries asked.

Ethan nodded and looking directly at the woman sitting at the panel table, he started walking toward her slowly, step by step, his eyes locked on hers, and recited a sonnet of Shakespeare's, and they let him speak it until he was finished.

She didn't look as if she could move, or speak, or even breathe. Her hand was on her heart and her eyes were wide, her lips slightly parted. The three men sitting with her looked at her in astonishment and then looked up at Ethan.

The man who had brought in the pastries nodded to him. "Thank you, that will be all," he said, and Ethan relaxed and gave them an easy smile, walking to them to shake each of their hands. He thanked them, and then left.

When the door closed behind Ethan, the four of them looked at each other.

"That's our guy," Murphy said, shaking his head. Valerie reached for her water and took a long drink of it.

Alex tilted his head at them and rubbed his chin. "He kind of looks like Thor, in a way, don't you think?"

"Fabio," Valerie said, refilling her water glass.

Jason frowned. "Who's Fabio?"

Valerie stared at him and Alex laughed. "He's Thor for romance book covers."

Murphy wiped pastry from his fingers. "Well, obviously he's a good looking guy, but he can act! I mean... what if we need him to lay it on thick? None of us could look away from him. He had us right in the palm of his hand. That's our guy."

Valerie frowned. "That might be our guy, but we had his bride-to-be narrowed down to these three ladies, and I like this one," she said, handing him a resume and photograph.

Murphy's brow lowered and he frowned slightly. "She's black."

Valerie just looked at him. "Yes, she is."

Murphy raised his eyebrows high. "She's gorgeous."

Valerie didn't blink. "Yes, she is."

Murphy looked at her then Jason and Alex. "Can she act?"

They both nodded seriously and Valerie smiled widely. "Like a charmer."

Murphy gave a thoughtful look at her photograph. "Haley Lawrence. Huh. She's a good one, that's for certain, and I trust your judgment implicitly." He raised his hand to his chin and rubbed it thoughtfully.

"You know, this could work. This could really work. Think about the conflict... and the ratings. Hang on. Let me make a call." Murphy reached for his phone.

He was one of the very few people who had Blaine Wright's phone number, and he almost never used it.

"Yes?" Blaine said shortly.

"Murphy here. Just finished the auditions and we have an idea for you. What about a mixed race couple. White groom, black bride. They are both gorgeous people and both talented actors. We think it would bring interesting conflict and just enough controversy to draw a bigger audience. We'd like to check with you first before we green light it." He was fairly sure he knew the answer, but in matters like this one, where the possible fate of a coming show was on the line, he knew it was always best to double check.

There was silence on the other end for a moment and Murphy knew Blaine was giving it serious consideration.

"Do it," Blaine said, and then hung up.
Murphy looked at the Holy Trinity sitting before him, their eyes locked on him waiting for an answer.

"Let's do it," he said with a grin, and all three of them smiled back up at him. "You call the girl. I'm going to call Thor back myself and tell him. Get them into the studio for separate contract meetings immediately, and remember that they can't see each other until the wedding. Tell them to choose their maid of honor and best man, and then I'll have the wedding crew dispatched to help them get ready for their big day."

"We'll do it!" Valerie said with a smile, and they stood up and began to pick up their belongings. Valerie took Haley's file and Murphy took Ethan's. Jason called an assistant from outside of the room to come take care of clean-up and dismiss the rest of the applicants for the audition.

Ethan was nearly home when his phone rang and he looked down at the unfamiliar number.

"This is Ethan," he said politely.

"Ethan, this is Murphy Newman. You were at an audition for my show today," Murphy began.

Ethan's heart began to thud against his chest as his eyes widened and he held his breath. It wasn't really happening. He wasn't actually getting a call back for the show...

"We want you for the part. I want to be sure about a few things before I start this," Murphy said seriously.

Ethan didn't know how he found his voice. "Of course, what can I help you with?"

"I want to be sure that you are single," Murphy said, wondering how a man that looked like Ethan did could possibly be single unless he was a player, which would make for an interesting season.

Ethan hesitated only a moment, hating the lie that he told. "I'm single."

Murphy continued. "You're going to be alright with marrying a complete stranger, no matter who she is, and then living with her in a home that we provide, until the end of the season? Also, we'll be filming you both from about seven every morning until ten at night every night, every day. You good with all of that?"

Ethan paused. "I would be leaving my whole life behind for this show, wouldn't I?" he asked cautiously.

"You would indeed," Murphy told him flatly.

Ethan sighed heavily. He hated to think of being away from Erica for even a few days, let alone nine long months. What on earth was he going to do without her? he wondered.

"Okay," Ethan said, sounding a little less convincing than he meant to. He was going to talk with Erica about it and try to talk her out of it, but he didn't want to lose the job in the meantime, just in case she really felt strongly about it.

"Come in to my office tomorrow morning at ten to sign the contract. I'll email the address to you." Murphy glanced over Ethan's contact information.

"Thank you for the call and the opportunity," Ethan said with a hollow voice. He meant it, but he wasn't at all sure that he was ready for a commitment like he was facing.

"Thank you for the Shakespeare today. It was well done and it was refreshing," Murphy told him with a smile.

They said goodbye and hung up and Ethan decided to go for a long walk through the park in his neighborhood. He gave the situation a great deal of thought and no matter how he turned it over and over in his mind, he kept coming back to one truth. It would be up to Erica in the end. He loved her. He would do anything for her.

He went back to the house and later that evening she came home, her hair tousled, looking tired and blissful.

Ethan rose up off the sofa and went to her, wrapping his arms around her and kissing her softly. He hugged her and stopped short for a moment, breathing in the scent at her neck. He leaned back and looked at her in confusion.

"Why do you smell like cologne?" he asked with a frown.

She rolled her eyes and pushed him away from her. "Oh you know, I was out running errands today and stopped by the nursing home to see my Uncle Randall. He likes to wear it to flirt with the nurses there. No big deal. He was sort of sweaty when I hugged him, and it rubbed off on me. I was just so busy running around that I didn't have time to wipe it off yet."

Ethan smiled at her. "You are so sweet to go visit him like you do. You're a good and caring niece. I'd love to meet him one day if it works out," he said, walking after her as she left him and went into the bedroom.

Erica walked into the bathroom and pulled her dress off, letting it fall to the floor at her feet before she reached for the sliding shower door.

Ethan frowned at her. "You went out without underwear on today? I thought you were wearing underwear this morning."

Erica didn't look at him. She ignored him, turned on the water, and got into the shower, closing the door behind her and calling out to him from beneath the stream. "I'll be out in a bit. I'll talk to you when I'm done in here. Shut the door behind you." He shrugged and walked into the bedroom, closing the bathroom door behind him.

She came out a short while later, nude and damp, toweling her thick red hair. Ethan could not take his eyes off her.

"How did the audition go?" she asked him curiously. "Did you make it in time? Did you get to go in front of anyone?"

He drew a deep breath and sighed. "I did make it in time, and I did audition, and they called me a while ago and I got the part." He spoke quietly, without enthusiasm, his eyes locked on her as she combed her hair. His groin tightened and ached for her.

Erica flipped around and grinned at him excitedly. "You got it! That's fantastic!" she got that far away look in her eyes and said, "Now I'll have all the money I need to get to New York and become a star!"

Then her eyes dropped to him and her smile began to fade as she saw the somber look on Ethan's face.

"What? What is that look for?" she asked, walking toward the bed in concern.

He sighed and shrugged. "I'll have to be away from you for nine whole months. They'd be filming me every day! I just don't want to be away from you for that long," he said sorrowfully.

Panic flashed across her face and then she smiled and crawled onto the bed with him, straddling her legs over his as she lowered herself slowly on top of him and kissed his mouth tenderly.

"Baby... don't talk like that. Don't try to back out on me now, now when I'm so close to my dream!" She kissed him deeply, pulling his hands to her breasts and then sliding hers down to his hardening groin. She stroked him and lifted her mouth from his to look intently at him.

"You've already come so far, now don't screw it up, come on baby, you have to do this for me. I need you to do it for me. I need that money. Go get it for me, baby." She lowered herself down to his erection and began to kiss and suck hard on him, making him breathless again.

"You love me, don't you?" she said just before she sucked on the tip of him and stroked him firmly.

He looked down at the beautiful woman pleasuring him and slid his fingers into her tangle of wet red hair, twisting his fingers in it snugly as he began to pump himself a little further into her mouth, letting the heat of desire flood through him.

"You know I love you more than anyone or anything," he gasped as he watched her tongue and her lips moving on him.

She pulled him from her mouth and moved upward to hover over him, teasing him with her body. She ran her hand slowly down his chest to his erection, where she closed her fingers around him and stroked him with one hand while she reached for a condom with the other. She pulled it onto him and smiled down at him as she slid him into her body.

"Then do this for me. I want it, baby," she told him as she began to sway gently on him. "I want it so bad. Give it to me." She kissed him hotly and he closed his hands around her huge breasts.

He ached at the thought of being away from her for such a long period of time. "Erica, it's almost a year without you. I just don't think I can-"

She closed his mouth with a sharp bite of her teeth and a hard hungry kiss afterward as her body began to move faster over his.

"It won't be that long. I'll come to you. We can have an affair... a hot affair... I'll be your other woman. I'll screw you in dark corners when no one is looking and you can see me then. Just don't mess this up for me. This is my big chance. You have to do it. You have to. You get your ass over to that show and earn that money for me, baby." She began to rock hard on him, reaching her hand up and pulling at fistfuls of his hair as she moved faster.

"Do it, baby. Get me that money. You'll see me in secret... we'll work it out. Come on... do it for me, lover," she said urgently as she thrust him into her fully.

Ethan cried out in pleasure and love, and held her close to him, kissing her tenderly. "I'll do it. Whatever you want, Erica, I'll do it, just don't make me be without you too long." He said it to her quietly as she closed her mouth over his and made him come hard.

The moment he began to relax and breathe, she moved off him and went to the bathroom. He laid in bed alone and a short while later she came back out to him and lay down near him.

He rolled over and looked at her back, reaching over to stroke her wild mane of hair and touch her skin.

"I would do anything for you, Erica. I love you. I just hate the idea of being away from you for so long."

She sighed and flipped over to face him and look at him. "So when do you leave?"

He finger combed her hair, pushing it off her bare body, moving it away from her face and tucking it behind her ear.

"I go sign the contract tomorrow, and then I think it will be pretty soon after that. Maybe less than a week." He felt empty just thinking about being without her that long. He gazed at her and then frowned as he saw something shining brightly beneath his fingers and he leaned up a little and looked at her ear. There was a massive diamond earring held in it.

"Wow, I haven't ever seen those before. When did you get those?" he asked her curiously, frowning in surprise.

She grinned smugly. "Oh, I just got those today. They were a little gift from Uncle Randall. The man has got some money and he loves to spoil me," she said happily.

Well, that was nice of him, Ethan thought, realizing that he wouldn't be meeting Uncle Randall for almost a year. "I hope he's still around at that old folks home when I get finished with this job."

Erica leaned up on her arms and looked at him seriously. "When you get finished with this job, we are going to New York. Period." Then she flipped her hair over her shoulder and her back and turned away from Ethan, settling herself for bed.

He stared at her a long while, watching her as she drifted off to sleep and thinking about how much he loved her. He would do anything in the world for her, even marry another woman he'd never met. Now, that had to be true love.

Chapter 3

The next morning, Haley put on a pretty summer dress and headed down to the studio where she was supposed to go sign the contract for the show. She felt nervous all morning, but when she saw the enormous building towering over the street and the city, her heart began to race even faster.

She entered the building and was cleared by the receptionist in the lobby, who sent her back behind the desk to take one of the secured elevators up to the fortieth floor. She rode up in the elevator alone, glancing around her for a moment at the polished brass and then looking straight ahead, staring at her reflection and telling herself that she looked beautiful and that she could handle whatever they may put in front of her.

The doors opened and her heart rate picked up again. She took a deep breath and walked out into a waiting room. There was another desk and another receptionist. This one looked to be expecting her.

"Good morning, Miss Lawrence. Please have a seat, Mr. Newman will be with you shortly. You're welcome to coffee and tea at the refreshment station there." She smiled before she went back to her phone.

Haley didn't feel like she could handle caffeine on top of her already jittery nerves, so instead she poured herself a glass of ice water and sat in a chair, waiting in the quiet room. The room didn't feel as contemporary as the rest of the building did; it was done in warmer colors, with thicker carpeting and more comfortable chairs than she had seen in the ground floor lobby, which was done more in steel and grey tones.

The ambiance in the room seemed to settle her nerves and ease her worries a little, until the receptionist came to her and told her that Mr. Newman was ready for her. Haley followed the receptionist through a doorway and down a hall that held several doors along the left and right sides.

At the end of the hall, the woman stopped and opened a door, smiling at Haley as Haley entered, and then the door closed behind her.

Off to the side of the room, in the corner where the glass walls of the exterior of the building met, stood a desk, and at it was a man with slightly slumped shoulders, and seriously thinning hair. He looked up at Haley and she smiled as their eyes met. His were a medium brown color, and though they held a sort of kindness, the kindness was overshadowed by something else, though Haley couldn't quite tell what it was.

"Good morning, Miss Lawrence. Thank you for coming in so early. Please have a seat." He invited her to sit at the chair before his desk.

She sat and smiled back at him. "Thank you, please call me Haley," she told him. He nodded and returned the pleasantry.

"Feel free to call me Murphy." He sat down opposite her. "Now, Haley, how much of this show concept are you familiar with? What is your understanding of it so far?" he asked, looking at her over his folded hands.

She sighed and thought about it. "I am going to be married to someone I don't know, and I'm going to try to stay married to him until the end of your show this season and if I do that, I'll be awarded one hundred thousand dollars."

Murphy nodded. "Okay. That's the general gist of it. Now, let's go over some of the finer details to it. We'll start with the immediate part. You will be signing the contract today, then you have three days to pack up whatever you want to take with you and see to your affairs, and then you will be taken to a hotel where you will stay for the three days leading up to your wedding.

"I have a wedding team picked out especially for you. They will be meeting you at the hotel and helping you get ready for your wedding. You'll be going to a spa, a salon, and the wedding shops to choose your dress, and the camera crew who will be with you for the duration of the season will be going with you on this initial expedition.

"I need you to choose your wedding colors today, by the way. I have a wedding crew who will be taking care of all of your wedding details, so there isn't anything else you need to do, unless you'd like to sit down with them and choose a few things like the cake and flowers. Do you have a preference about those?"

He paused and waited for her to speak.

She felt like she was sitting in the middle of a whirlwind. She realized when he asked her, that she didn't care at all what they did with the wedding. She had always thought that she would plan her own wedding to a man that she loved, and it would be one of the most wonderful days of her life. But it wasn't happening like that, and as she was marrying someone that she didn't know, she had to admit that it didn't feel in the least like she was preparing for a real wedding.

"No, you can do whatever you want to for the wedding," she told him.

Murphy nodded. "Good, fine. Now, there are a few notes that I want to make sure you're aware of. No one you know will be at the wedding, but you may have a maid of honor there if you like. If you don't have one, we'll provide one for you."

She immediately thought of Leslie. Leslie was the one who had gotten her into this situation in the first place. "I have one," she told him and he nodded.

"When the wedding is over, you'll both be living together in a home that we provide. It's already going to be furnished and decorated, so you two just have to move in together and bring your personal things. If you want to redecorate the house or make any changes to it, that's fine. No need to check in with us about that.

"We'll have the camera crew in with you every day from seven in the morning until ten at night, or until you go to bed. Except for Sundays, when everyone is off camera. Now, your resume says that you are currently working at a real estate company. Are you planning on keeping that job?" he asked pointedly.

She shrugged. "I am looking for another job," she told him honestly.

He nodded. "You will be paid a moderate sum for doing this show. Sort of a stipend, but a little more than what is usually considered a stipend. As the show is covering your living expenses at the house, you won't have that many debts, and so you may be able to stop working if you like, and focus on the show full time. That is the only thing that will affect the camera crew's schedule. If you and your future husband are both at work, that would mean that the camera crew would be off during your working hours, but if you are at home, then they'd need to be there with you."

Haley tilted her head curiously. "Is my husband going to be working during the day?" she asked.

Murphy rubbed his hand over his lower lip thoughtfully for a moment. "You aren't allowed to know anything about him until after the wedding, so bring that question back up again later. For now we will just say that you should decide whether or not you will be working out of the home or staying home, and let me know, as I'll need to schedule the camera crew around it.

"We're only going to air the good material, things people are interested in seeing, but there will be no time where you are not in front of the lens, except Sundays. If you choose to stay home, that's fine. If you choose to work outside of the home, that's fine too. Just let me know."

Haley thought about it. If the money was the same or more than she was making at the realtor's office, then she probably could stay home because she wouldn't have any of the overhead living expenses that she currently had. She would put out an ad to sublet her apartment and transfer all of the utilities to someone else. She wouldn't have many debts at all after that, and she might well be able to stay at home and actually do some of her painting and artwork.

"I think I'm going to try to stay at the house, if I can manage it. I'm an artist and I just haven't had time to do anything artistic, and I feel like this would be a good opportunity for me to get back into my artwork."

He looked at her seriously and made some notes on the pages in a file before him. "I wasn't aware that you are an artist. That's good to know." He wrote a few more things down and then looked at her again.

"You'll have limited contact with your family and friends as we want you to spend the majority of your time getting to know your husband. The idea of the show is to see if arranged marriages can work out into true love. We have a limited amount of time to see how that works for you both and we want to give it everything that we can to see if it will be a success. Does that work for you?" he asked, looking at her directly.

His expression was unreadable.

She felt her heart catch. Limited contact with family and friends. They wanted to know if they could make her fall in love with a stranger in a specified time frame. She suddenly felt like a rat in a science lab. There was a hundred thousand dollars at the end of it, she reminded herself. There was money to be had; money that could enable her to really get her art career going. She just had to get through the handful of months leading up to the spring. She told herself that it wasn't that different than going off to college or something like it.

"I guess it will have to," she answered him. It was going to have to work. "I am committed to it, it might be a little difficult, but I can do it," she assured him with as much confidence as she could muster.

He eyed her carefully and nodded. "Alright then, here is the contract. Please go ahead and read through it and sign it for me in all the areas that are indicated."

He handed her a thick packet of pages and then rose from his desk, walking toward the door. "I have some phone calls to make, but I'll just be down the hall if you have any questions about it."

Murphy left, and Haley looked at the first page and began reading. It was a lot more commitment than she thought she was going to have to go through, but by the time she got to the end of it, she thought that she could probably handle it.

She signed it and set it on his desk, feeling as if she had just signed away her entire life. Haley drew a deep breath and let it go, hoping her anxiety would go with it, and then she stood up and walked out of Murphy's office.

She found him near the receptionist's desk, his phone held up to his ear. He saw her and she waited as he ended his call and then looked at her expectantly.

"Did you have any questions?" he asked her.

She shook her head. "No, I read it all and understood it. Basically I'm selling my soul to you." She told him that a little tongue in cheek, but then she smiled.

He raised his eyebrows and tilted his head. "Yeah, basically that's exactly what you are doing. Well, get packed up and get your affairs settled. I'll send a car to pick you up in three days. Then it's off to get the wedding dress." He smiled at her and reached his hand out to her.

She shook it and then went back to the elevators, wondering just how different her life was going to be. When she got out to her car, she called Leslie.

Leslie answered right away. "Well? What's going on?"

"I'm calling you to see if you will be my maid of honor. I'm getting married pretty soon and I'd love for you to be there, since this whole thing is your doing, anyway," she said with a half teasing voice.

Leslie squealed. "Yay! That's so exciting! Of course I will. I'll be glad to do that for you. So, when do we get ready for that part?" she asked curiously.

"Well," Haley sighed, "first I have to take care of getting my place sublet, and then I have to pack. I'll need help with that, if you're free," she said hopefully.

"I'm free! I will come and help you, of course."
"Thanks, Leslie." Haley smiled. "I go to the hotel in three days and from there it's wedding stuff and then moving into the house. I guess we'll see how it goes."

"Well, I am going to help you with whatever you need, you just let me know. We'll have you married off in no time. Just let me know when I need to start looking for divorce lawyers." She laughed.

"Now.... probably." Haley laughed. "I'll be at the house all afternoon taking care of things. Come over anytime you want to."

"See you soon!" Leslie grinned through the phone.

**

Ethan stepped out of the elevator and the receptionist at the desk looked up from her computer and almost did a double take. She grinned at him and her eyes sparkled. He smiled pleasantly. Most women treated him that way, and he took it in stride. He wasn't one to take advantage of the way that women automatically wanted to cater to him, but sometimes it did come in handy, as long as it wasn't harmful to anyone.

"My name is Ethan. I'm here to see Murphy Newman."

The receptionist nodded blithely and picked up her phone. "Mr. Newman? Yes... there's a gentleman here by the name of Ethan to see you."

"Please feel free to take your time," she told him before hanging up and returning her attention to Ethan.

"He'll be out in just a minute," she said, looking up at him through her eyelashes.

"Thanks." Ethan turned to walk to the chairs. The receptionist hopped up from her seat and hurried around the desk to him.

"Can I get you a coffee or tea? Some water... while you wait? Anything at all?" she asked, weaving her fingers together near her stomach.
He looked back at her for a moment and shook his head. His long blonde hair was spilling over his shoulder. "No thanks, I'm fine."

He sat down and she took a few more steps toward him. "I could get you something to read if you like, or... there are cookies in the back. Do you like sweet things?" she asked with a grin.

Ethan looked up at her and smiled slightly, shaking his head. "I'm okay, thank you, though."

She nodded and stood in place, staring at him with a grin on her face.

There was an awkward silence and then he looked up at her.

"Are you doing a show or a movie with Mr. Newman?" she asked cordially.

He shrugged slightly. "I'm not sure if I can answer that question."

She nodded and waved her hands. "Sorry, I wouldn't want to get you into trouble."

Ethan knew she wasn't going to leave him alone. "Please don't let me keep you from your work, I'm sure you're a very busy lady." He smiled at her kindly.

Her smile faltered and she nodded a little. "I am a little busy," she said, her shoulders falling slightly

Murphy walked into the room and looked at them both. "Ethan! Glad you could come. Please come back to the office. Maryanne... shouldn't you be at the desk?" He frowned at her slightly and she blushed and went back to her seat.

Ethan waved at her as he followed Murphy, and she perked up and grinned, waving back.

Murphy took him to the last office down the hall and sat across the desk from him. He explained everything about the show and the contract that he had explained to Haley, and Ethan frowned at him.

"I have... family... that I would want to see as often as I could," Ethan said, lying a little. Erica was practically his family. She was his girlfriend.

Murphy shook his head. "Not going to happen often. We are keeping the contact between the two of you and the people in your regular lives down to a bare minimum. We have to try to see if the two of you will fall in love with each other during the term of the season. If you're distracted with family and friends outside of the program, it may detract from that happening."

Ethan didn't like the idea at all. He wanted to tell Murphy to give the role to someone else, but Erica's beautiful face came into his mind... her beautiful, determined, insistent face. She had reminded him that morning how important it was to her that he see this plan through, that he get the hundred thousand dollars for her, and that he not back out of it and not fail.

She had rocked his world that morning, showing her love for him in the only way she ever did... and it felt so good that he had to make himself swear that he wouldn't let her down. He loved her, she was his, and he would do anything for her. He had promised. It was so important to her.

"So you have four days to pack up and then I'll have a car come pick you up at the hotel. You'll be at the hotel for two days and then we'll have the wedding and then the two of you will move into your new home together. Take whatever you think you'll want with you for nine months. Almost everything the two of you do will be done together." he said, making it a solid point.

Ethan nodded quietly and Erica's face played through his mind. "Alright. Where do I sign?" he asked.

Murphy pulled out the contract and handed it to him. He skimmed through it and signed on all of the lines, and then he looked up at Murphy.

"That's it, Ethan. I'll send the car in four days," Murphy said simply.

Ethan nodded and stood up, reaching to shake Murphy's hand before he turned to leave the office.

Maryanne nearly pounced on him as he entered the reception area and headed for the elevators.

"Hi, Ethan, listen, if you need anything at all, if you want any help or... anything, I just want you to know that I'm here for you and you have my support. Here's my number. Call me if you need anything!" she told him, pressing a slip of paper into his hand. "Ever!" she added.

He smiled and nodded and was grateful when the elevator doors closed between them and blocked the view of her gazing at him, batting her eyes and smiling hugely.

Ethan went home and realized that he would have to pack enough for nearly a year. He carefully selected the things he knew he'd want, while others were tucked away to be kept for later. Erica wasn't home. He wanted to tell her how it had all gone, that he had signed the paperwork and that it was all official, but she wasn't to be found.

Leslie spent all three days with Haley, helping her pack and clean, helping her choose a renter to sublet her apartment while she was gone, and enjoying every moment of her best friend's company that she was able to until it was time for Haley to go.

She was in the bathroom, singing and packing a box of the contents of the medicine cabinet behind the mirror and the shelves and drawers beneath the sink, when Haley came to her and leaned over her, gently taking hold of her arm.

Haley wrapped a pretty pearl bracelet around Leslie's arm and fastened it and Leslie's mouth fell open in surprise before she grinned and squealed, looking at it.

"It's so pretty! Thank you!" she said happily. "What on earth is it for?"

"I just wanted to find a way to thank you for all that you've done for me. You're such an amazing friend, and I just want you to know that I love you and I appreciate you more than you will ever know. That's all."

Leslie hauled herself up off the bathroom floor and hugged Haley.

"I'm going to miss you so much. I know it's going to fly by and you'll be back around in no time, but in the meantime, it's going to feel like forever! Call me as often as you can. Promise?" she asked.

Haley frowned slightly. "I don't get much communication with friends and family; they really want to try to push the husband and me into falling for one another. It's their goal. They think that friends and family will be a distraction from that, so communication is limited, but when I can talk with you, I definitely will. I'm going to miss you too, so much!" She grinned and hugged her friend again.

They spent the three days getting ready, laughing, planning, and enjoying each other, and then on the third day a limousine pulled up to the apartment and they hugged each other goodbye tightly, tears fell, and they smiled and waved at one another as the limo pulled away.

Four days after he went to sign his contract, Ethan was packed and ready to go. Erica hadn't come home the night before; she said she had a friend who needed her and she had to stay the night with her friend. He had hoped to see more of her before he left, but she was gone most of the four days he had been home packing and getting ready to leave. She had been spending a lot of time visiting Uncle Randall who was spoiling her with lots of expensive gifts. He had tried to call her so he could see her before he left, but her phone was off.

She probably forgot to charge it, he thought to himself. He sent her a text and told her that he would be at the house until noon, and then the car was coming to pick him up to go to the hotel, and he wouldn't see her for a long time. He hoped it would encourage her to come home sooner, but as he sat and waited and the clocked ticked slowly ahead, he began to realize that she wasn't going to be there in time.

Taking a pen and paper, he wrote her a lengthy love letter, telling her how much he loved her, how much she meant to him, and that he would miss her while he was off doing the work it would take to earn the award money for her so she could get to New York.

The limousine pulled up in front of his apartment and he left the letter on her pillow and took a long last look at the home they shared, knowing he would miss it tremendously, and miss her more than anything.

He picked up his bag and walked out, closing and locking the door behind him.

   ***

Haley was delivered to the hotel and was allowed to spend her first half-day there relaxing and settling in, but as she slept soundly the next morning, she was roused by a sharp knock at her bedroom door.

She sat up abruptly, sheets falling away, pillows tumbling as she looked around. "Who is it?" she asked.

"Your team! We brought coffee!" It was a woman's voice.

The wedding team. Haley had forgotten they were coming so early. She looked at the clock. It was eight o'clock, right on the button. She sighed, rubbed her face for a moment, and then answered the door.

She was wearing a tank top and shorts and as she pulled the door wide, three people filed in; two women and a man, and the woman in front was indeed carrying coffee that tugged invitingly at Haley's nose and mouth.

The man was wearing a fine linen shirt and pants with leather shoes. He had a bald head and wore designer sunglasses. He smiled at her and pulled the sunglasses off, revealing bright blue eyes.

"Well hello, darling, aren't you a lovely little thing!" he told her, his hand going straight to his hip as he cocked his head flamboyantly.

Haley smiled and blushed a little. "Thank you. I'm Haley Lawrence," she told him, reaching her hand out to him. He took it and made a little cross between a bow and a curtsy to her.

"I'm Sage and this Andrea," he said, indicating the woman to his left who was wearing a stylish pantsuit, "and Portia." Portia was wearing a little black dress that managed to look professional and sexy at the same time.

Portia handed her a cup of coffee. "Do you like sugar or cream?" she asked sweetly.

Haley was surprised by them; they looked like they had just stepped out of some international fashion magazine, but they also looked like they knew how to have a lot of fun.

"Cream please." She smiled. Andrea handed her some creamer to go with her coffee.

Sage looked her up and down. "Well my dear, you need to get ready as soon as you finish your java, because we have got a lot to do in the next two days! Don't worry too much about a hairstyle or makeup, because our first stop is a spa. Then we're off to the salon. I can hardly wait! It's going to be so exciting!" He clapped his hands together.

Haley sipped her coffee and smiled, it was cinnamon hazelnut and it tasted incredible. She knew she was going to love her time with her prep team.

"Now, dearest, you have to hurry, because the camera crew will be here in no time to film you going from single to married, and you just can't see them looking like this. The nation will be watching you! You have to show them your best side. We want them to be enthralled with you! Off you go now..." he lightly touched her shoulders and turned her toward the bathroom.

She laughed a little and went to shower and dress. A short while later she was ready to go, and as she emerged from the bathroom, she found her prep team sitting in her room waiting to go, and excited to help her.

Sage rose from the chair he was sitting in and lifted his hands in the air. "Let's go make a bride!" he said happily, and all the women followed him out of the room.

They rode in the limousine to the spa and the camera crew met them when they arrived. Haley stepped out of the limousine and the prep team introduced her to the two men who would be her camera crew for the next nine months.

The taller, slightly older one stepped forward and extended his hand, smiling at her. "Hello Miss Lawrence, I'm Harvey Corman. Glad to be working with you. This is my sound guy, Joe Davidson." He introduced the small thin man standing beside him wearing a grin, glasses, and a baseball cap. They both seemed like very nice men, Haley decided.

"It's so nice to meet you both. I am completely new at this, so any advice or thoughts you have about what I'm doing would be so appreciated!"

They both nodded and promised her they'd take good care of her.

"You're our girl; we're going to make sure you are shown in the best possible way,"
Harvey told her. "To start with, we're going to ask you to exit your limo again so we can get arrival

footage, and then we will follow you into the spa,"
he told her, picking up his camera.

She agreed and climbed back into the limo. Harvey
waved at the limo driver, he opened the door of the
car, and Haley and her crew climbed out, smiling at
the camera. She waved at the lens and talked about
how excited she was to get pampered for her big day.

The entourage followed her in and filmed moments of
her getting steamed, massaged, and waxed, covered in
sea mud and hidden beneath the layers of her facial.
She walked out of the spa feeling like a new woman,
and she was definitely more relaxed.

The next stop was the salon. Two stylists worked on
her simultaneously, and the camera crew was there
filming as she had her hair washed, colored, cut, and
styled. She had a pedicure and a manicure, as well as
her makeup. Sage would be styling it on her wedding
day at the hotel, but he was adamant that this
preparatory visit to the salon was more than necessary
for her.

By the time she walked out, she looked more
glamorous than she had ever looked in her life and
she was beyond thrilled about it.

She looked at Sage and grinned and he blew her a
kiss.

"Amazing, darling, you look simply unbelievable!" he
promised her, taking her hand in his arm.

"So now what are we doing?" she asked excitedly.

He looked at her with raised brows, "We are getting lunch and then we are moving on to the big part of the day. We are going to get your wedding dress."

Leslie met the team at the first wedding dress shop and then rode with them the rest of the day, trying on bridesmaid dresses.

Three stores and four hours later, they were surrounded by several possible wedding dress options. There were two that Haley really loved, and after trying them both on twice with varying opinions, she finally opted for the strapless white satin gown with the sweetheart neckline, gathered sides, fitted waist and mermaid flare from the knee down.

Sage proclaimed her exquisite, while Leslie, Andrea, and Portia all applauded at the decision. The camera crew got it all. Even Joe and Harvey both approved of the gown.

They all agreed on a dress for Leslie and Andrea sent still photographs of the dresses to the florist who was working on the flowers for them.

"That's going to make for a really good lead up to the show. We're going to get this on the air tonight!" Joe told her.

It was surreal and dizzying to think that the whole nation would be watching commercial previews of her going through the day she had just had. Spa, salon, lunch, shopping for wedding dresses.

"Is the groom going through any of this?" she asked curiously. "Does he have a team, too?"

Harvey shook his head. "No, we do a little bit of sneaky preview work with him, but not anything close to this. He's not revealed until the day of the wedding, you know, to keep everyone guessing. Everyone meets you first, and then all of you meet the groom on your wedding day."

She looked at him intently and asked in a quiet voice, "Is he nice? Is he a good guy?"

Harvey bit his lip and looked at her with a shake of his head. "I'm not allowed to tell you anything about him."

Haley sighed. "I understand. I'm just so... nervous." she told him with a small smile.

Harvey watched her silently for a moment and then said, "If you were my sister, I would be okay with you marrying him. That's the best I can give you."

Her eyes lit up and she smiled brightly, and he grinned back at her and patted her back. "It's going to be a good season, I think."

She certainly hoped so. She knew it was going to be a defining year of her life. She just hoped that it would be a good one. Leaving everything behind, getting married, and trying for a hundred grand was way out of her realm of reality, or at least, it was before Leslie told her about the ad.

They got the dress, the shoes, the veil, and the jewelry, which was loaned to the show from a jewelry store who was keen on being featured alongside the bridal store before the public eye.

Shopping and pampering finished, they all went to dinner together, and then parted ways. Leslie hugged Haley tight and told her that everything was going to be amazing. Haley hoped so, but she was going into it blind, so hope was basically all that she had.

Two days later, she hadn't gotten hardly any sleep at all and she was feeling more nervous than ever. Her prep team knocked on the door and came in with a big breakfast cart for her when she opened the door to them and her camera crew, who Sage would not allow to film her until he had some of her base makeup applied.

Sage took one look at her and rolled his eyes, sitting her down on the edge of her bed.

"You didn't sleep, did you?" he asked with a heavy sigh, reaching behind him and picking up a bottle of champagne. He opened it as she bit her lip and shook her head no.

He poured the champagne into a glass and then topped it off with orange juice. "Well, darling, this isn't going to be the most important day of your life but you do have to look the part, so drink this up, eat a croissant, and then we'll get to work on you."

Two more mimosas and two chocolate filled croissants later, she was feeling a little better, and her team was working hard on her hair and makeup. They had her looking like a runway model in a couple of hours, and then they helped her into her dress, shoes, and veil.

They stood her in front of the mirror and she was shocked. She had never seen herself look so good. She teared up a little and Sage shook his finger at her. "You aren't allowed to cry. You'll destroy my masterpiece and you look stunning, so stop it. Now. Remember that you are a fairytale princess today and just live in that knowledge. You are walking down the aisle to your prince, and your life is going to be happy ever after. Just focus on that," he told her.

Haley nodded and he handed her one more mimosa, which she downed swiftly, and then he handed her an elegant bouquet of flowers.

"These are Vera Wang. Carry them like they are made of glass." he told her, straightening the bouquet in her hand.

She nodded subtly. Pretend to be a princess walking to her prince. Carry the flowers like they are glass. Happy ever after. One hundred thousand dollars.

Haley followed her team downstairs to a long hallway and partway down the hall they turned her and walked out of a door into a garden with a long white carpet laid out before her. It was strewn with light lavender, white, and peach colored rose petals.

She turned suddenly and looked at Sage and Portia. Andrea had already hurried to her seat.

"I can't do this. I'm going to throw up," she said in a panicked voice.

Sage lifted his chin and closed his eyes as he shook his head. "Hush." Then he looked at her earnestly. "Of course you can do this. You are acting. It's a job. A very good paying job. You are 'on camera' for a while, that's it. You most certainly can do it. Just remember that it's a job. You are being paid to be a princess who is marrying her prince. It's just acting... acting real; it is a reality show, but it's still just acting. You can do it. If you couldn't do it, they'd never have chosen you. There were thousands of women who wanted this role. You can do it. So do it."

He leaned over and kissed her cheek, then turned her and gave her a little push. "Count to thirty and then start walking down that aisle."

Portia squeezed her hand and then the two of them disappeared to join Andrea.

Haley closed her eyes and counted slowly to thirty. Then she took a deep breath, opened her eyes and began to walk down the aisle.

When she rounded a corner in the garden, she heard live music playing and she felt her heartbeat quicken. The camera crew had only filmed part of her dressing, makeup, and styling preparation before they went to the hallways to film her walking to the altar. They were stationed near the altar, and there was another team she could see filming the groom.

He stood with his back to her as he was instructed to do. She saw his back and saw that he had long blonde hair to his shoulders and she did her best not to let the shock that rocked through her register on her face. She looked at Leslie who was standing near the altar waiting for her, and Leslie grinned and winked. *That had to be a good sign*, she thought. She lifted her chin and walked, all eyes on her save her future husband's, and three cameras were on her as she looked straight ahead and smiled widely, stopping when she reached the end of the aisle.

The officiant nodded and she turned to look at her husband to be.

Ethan felt her next to him, and when he turned to look at her, he could not hide the surprise on his face. She was gorgeous, and she was nothing at all like the woman he had assumed they would probably have him marry. Her hair was pulled up and twisted in curls around her head, almost like a crown. Her skin was dark creamy mocha, her eyes were sea green, and she was unquestionably one of the most beautiful women he had ever seen in his life. He hoped her personality matched her looks.

She looked as surprised as he did, and she felt it. There before her was a tall, gorgeous, blonde, white man, who was practically a wall of muscle. She was shocked at the interracial choice they had made, but not at all disappointed with it. He was a beautiful man, no question about it, but as she looked into his hazel eyes, she could see that his heart was no more invested in their scheme than hers was. She took note of that and smiled big for the cameras, which encouraged him to do the same.

Both of them recovered and the music silenced.

As the officiant read their vows, their hearts raced, and they repeated to each other the promises he spoke for them. The man asked them for the rings. Haley turned to Leslie who gave her a thrilled grin and took her bouquet as she handed her a golden band for Ethan.

Ethan took the ring from his best man and then they exchanged them. She was surprised and delighted at the pretty diamond ring he put on her finger. It wasn't big, but it was beautifully designed, and it sparkled in the sunlight against her skin.

They were pronounced man and wife and Ethan hesitated only a moment before placing his hands tentatively on her waist, leaning down, and kissing her gently. His kiss was warm and soft, and then it was gone and he smiled lightly at her.

She couldn't believe it. She was married. Legally married to a complete stranger. They turned and their crews clapped and cheered for them. Bubbles were blown thickly as they walked down the aisle together, and the camera crew followed them into a courtyard in the garden, near where they had just had their ceremony.

There was a beautifully decorated table with a three tiered wedding cake and champagne flutes. The bubbly was poured, the best man and maid of honor faked toasts to the couple, and then Ethan and Haley held the knife together and cut into their cake. Each of them slipped a piece of it into the other's mouth, carefully and politely. They sipped their champagne and then Murphy, who was standing there beside Blaine, both of them off camera, waved to the couple to kiss again.

Ethan sighed. He knew there would be several months of this. If he wanted that money for Erica, he knew he'd better make it look real and sell this ridiculous show to the nation at large. So, he slid his hands around Haley's waist and held her close to him, leaning down and kissing her tenderly for a long moment before letting her go.

The cameras were finally turned off, the cake was passed out to the show crew and producers. Haley was a little surprised to see the three people that she had auditioned for come up for cake.

She and Ethan looked at each other and he put his hand out to her.

"I'm Ethan, by the way, Ethan Richards." He gave her a genuine smile.

"Haley Lawrence." She responded. "It's nice to meet you," she told him with a little laugh.

Harvey and Joe were standing beside them and saw the exchange, and both of them smiled.

Ethan and Haley were introduced to the Holy Trinity, Blaine, and some of the other writers and producers for the show who had been the guests at their wedding. It was a completely surreal experience for them.

Haley stayed as near to Leslie as she could, though Leslie and Alex Moran had taken a liking to each other and had spent a good portion of time talking and eventually exchanging phone numbers.

"He's one of the guys I auditioned for," Haley whispered to Leslie when she finally had her ear.

"I know! He told me he did the auditions with that lady, Valerie, and the other guy, Jason. Alex is so amazing. I hope he calls me!" She grinned and winked at Haley.

Haley laughed at her and shook her head.

Murphy came up to Haley and Ethan, had them sign the marriage documents and then handed them a set of keys, which Joe and Harvey filmed.

"Welcome to your new life, Mr. and Mrs. Richards. You'll be going straight to the house from here when the party is over," he told them. "Filming begins immediately."

They nodded and Haley forced herself not to be sick.

Possibly out of nervousness, they prolonged the party as much as they could, but Murphy finally ushered them out amidst handshakes, congratulations, and wishes of luck.

Haley's last view of Leslie was with Alex's arm wrapped close around her, and then the limo pulled away from the hotel, and she sat still for a moment and then turned and looked at Ethan.

"Well..." she said with a quiet voice. "Here we go."

He smiled a little and nodded. "Here we go."

Chapter 4

The car pulled up to the house and he helped her out onto the sidewalk. They stood there together, looking at the home that they would be sharing for the next nine months. It was a single story ranch home with a good-sized front yard and a small front porch. There were varying angles at the front; it wasn't a flat walled front, but rather it appeared to be broken in large squares of varying shapes and sizes, with several windows that overlooked the street. A porch swing hung near the door.

There were palm trees in the yard and a paved sidewalk. There was a mailbox, and on the side of it, letters read, 'Richards'. It struck Haley that it was all too real, all too fast. She felt her heart pound against her chest and she drew her breath in, suddenly afraid, but Ethan heard her and reached his hand to her back to steady her.

She looked up at him in panic and saw an assurance in his hazel eyes. He nodded to her and then looked back at the intimidating edifice before them, took her hand, and walked her to the front door. She followed, and was grateful for his support, because at that moment, she had no strength in the world and had been one heartbeat from turning and running down the street, money or not.

His hand was closed warmly around hers as they reached the door, and his strength and confidence seemed to flow from him into her so that when he paused after opening the door and then bent to pick her up suddenly, carrying her over the threshold, she laughed in spite of everything, and her laugh drew his attention. He looked at her with a genuine smile and for a fraction of a moment, even he felt that, perhaps somehow, they would both get through it all.

The film crew was capturing every bit of their new life; the entrance to their new home, the tour of it as they walked through it, and every nuance that passed between them. Joe and Harvey were on it.

There was a large, bright sunny dining room immediately to the left of the doorway, and a living room to the right, and all throughout the home there were hardwood floors. Beyond that, towards the back of the home was a study that led into a hallway that was the main vein of the house. Behind the dining room to the left was the kitchen; it was a large room with marble counter tops, new stainless steel appliances, and an island in the center of the cooking area. Further back from the cooking area was a breakfast nook, and a full glass wall that opened to a garden and the back yard.

A side door to the kitchen led to another area of the home where there were two bedrooms; one a guest bedroom, and one a master bedroom with a doorway to the house, and a double doorway to the backyard where they found a pool and Jacuzzi. Beyond the pool was a small structure big enough to hold a single car but designed instead as a closed-in space with two windows looking toward the house, and a door to walk into it.

"That's interesting." Haley said as she began to walk to it.

Ethan walked up to it, opened the door and looked in, and then closed the door and looked at Haley. "It's mine," he said resolutely. "It's going to be my man cave."

She looked at him in shock. "What?" she asked in surprise.

He stood there looking at her seriously. "I get the shed. It's my place. You can have the rest of the house. That's my spot. I don't want you to come out and get into it, I just want it for myself. I think that's a fair request."

Haley couldn't even begin to think of what to say to him so she just shrugged and shook her head. "Alright. I guess so," she said with a disapproving tone.

They walked back into the house and went to their room, where they found a large bed and matching bedroom furniture waiting for them. Haley stopped and stared at the bed for a moment, realizing that they were going to be sleeping together in that same bed. Every night. For nine months. It was yet another thing that made panic rush through her veins.

"Would you like the bathroom first?" she asked, looking at him as he was putting his clothes into one side of the dresser.

He shrugged. "Okay."

While he showered, she put her own clothes in the other half of the dresser and closet. She had brought pajamas that were more conservative, not even realizing that they would be sharing a bed, and it made her feel relief that she'd had the foresight to do it. She selected a pair that consisted of a soft pink tank top and soft satin pants for the bottoms.

By the time Ethan stepped out of the shower, she was completely unpacked in their bedroom. He walked out in nothing but shorts and she stared at him for a moment, at his wet golden hair hanging tousled over his shoulders and his ripped body as he walked toward the bed. She caught her breath for a moment and then looked away, not wanting either of them to feel awkward. The camera crew was in the room with them, catching all of it.

He looked at her and said simply, "The bathroom is all yours." and then he went to bed.

Haley walked into the bathroom and was immediately annoyed. Perhaps it was because she had lived alone for a while, she thought, but when she found his clothes discarded on the floor, the toothpaste tube squeezed in the middle with the cap off, water everywhere and a damp towel crumpled in the corner by the tub, she was not happy at all.

Her first thought was to say something to him, but then she thought better of it, before she spoke. It had been a long day. Perhaps he was just overly tired. Perhaps he hadn't meant to be messy and inconsiderate. She picked up his towel and hung it to dry. She picked up his clothes and put them into the hamper. She wiped up the water everywhere and put the toothpaste away after using it.

Then she showered and put her own pajamas on, and walked out into the bedroom, wondering what she would find. She found the camera crew waiting, and Ethan snoring away on his pillow.

Haley looked at Harvey and Joe. "I think that's all you're going to get tonight, guys," she said with a smile. "Thank you for all of your hard work."

They nodded and then walked out and told her they would lock the front door behind them.

Haley crawled into bed wondering how her life was going to be for the next several months. She had moderate hopes for success, but not much more than that. All she could think of to make herself feel better, was the money at the end. Then she could open her own gallery.

In the days that followed, Haley soon found out exactly what it would be like living with Ethan, and so did the rest of the country. It turned out that he wasn't just tired on their wedding night, he was just an unkempt roommate, and after two weeks of alternating between ignoring it and hoping that it would encourage him to pick up after himself and picking up after him because he wouldn't pick up after himself, she had finally had enough.

She lost her temper one day when she found his wet swimming trunks on her side of the bed. They had left a wide circle on most of the bed soaked with pool water, and she knew there was no way that it was going to be dry by the time she wanted to go to sleep.

Harvey and Joe had been watching them battle silently with one another over the house cleaning, and they were ready when Haley lost her cool. The camera was rolling when she snapped.

"Ethan!" she yelled, standing beside the bed, holding his shorts up.

There was no answer.

"ETHAN!" she hollered again.

Still no answer. She grabbed his shorts in her hand and stalked out to the back yard where she thought that he was probably hiding in his man cave. She banged her fist on the door and a few moments later, he opened it and gave her an unpleasant look.

"What?" he asked her with a frown.

"You did it again! I can't believe how thoughtless you are!" she said angrily at him.

He came out of the shed fully and closed the door behind him. "What are you talking about?" he asked in confusion.

She thrust his wet shorts at him and he stared at her. "What are you doing with my shorts?"

"You left them on my side of the bed and now the whole bed is soaking wet with nasty pool water! It's not going to be dry tonight and we're going to have to sleep in the guest room!" she snapped at him.

"Just blow dry it," he told her with a shrug. "You don't have to get so worked up about it." He shook his head.

She narrowed her eyes at him. "Blow dry the bed. Are you kidding me? That water has soaked through the mattress. There's no way it's going to be dry even if I do try to blow dry it! It's going to take two or three days for that to air out! You're so inconsiderate of everything all of the time!" She raised her voice and Harvey and Joe came in a little closer to them.

"How am I inconsiderate?" he asked in irritation, his own temper beginning to flare.

She looked at him in complete shock. "You must be joking. Are you serious? You don't know?" Her hands were on her hips and her voice was sharp as a razor.

"No, I don't know. Why don't you tell me?" He lowered his brows at her and frowned.

She shook her head at him. "You leave the toilet seat up all the time, you leave your dirty clothes and wet towels all over the place and you don't put your clean clothes away!" she started with the short list of reasons she was mad at him.

"What business is it of yours what I do with my clothes?" he snapped back at her.

"It's my business because I have to live here with you, too! I have to trip over them, or pick them up so they don't mildew and mold, or put them in the dryer after you've left them in the washer all day, or put them in the hamper so they can be washed! That's not all of it though, not by a long shot! There are so many things you do!

"You leave dirty dishes in the sink, you never load or clean out the dishwasher. You leave uneaten food around, you leave the remote control all over the house so I never know where it is. You track dirt in with your shoes instead of leaving your shoes by the front door in the basket that I put there. You never help me cook, you don't do any of the cleaning, you always leave the lid off of the toothpaste, and you smoke cigars in the house! It reeks in there! You insisted on this man cave out here, so smoke your stinky old cigars out here!" she yelled at him. "And take care of your clothes!" she shouted as she threw his soaking wet shorts at him and turned around and stomped off.

"Yeah? Well, you're no treat to live with either!" He called out after her, but she was already gone back inside the house, slamming the door behind her.

Joe looked at Harvey and Harvey smiled. "I bet you a hundred bucks they don't make it to the New Year."

Joe looked at Ethan and then at the back door and laughed, shaking his head. "I'll take that bet. I think they're going to make it past the season."

Ethan looked at them and almost growled. "I'm not sure we're going to make it past this week!" he grumbled and went back into his man cave.

Neither of them was speaking to the other one when they went to bed in the guest room that night. Haley was right, the bed was soaking wet, and no amount of blow drying was going to dry it in time for them to sleep on it that night or the next.

The bed in the guest room was smaller, and they were forced to sleep closer to one another, neither of them liking it, and both of them silently angry about it, which Harvey and Joe got on film.

They also filmed Ethan without his knowledge, when he called Erica from the man cave shortly after the fight. She answered after several rings and the sound of her voice filled Ethan with monumental happiness.

"Babe! Oh God, I'm so glad to hear you... I miss you so much. How are you doing?" he asked, anxious to hear almost anything from her.

"I'm great. Look, why are you calling me? Aren't you supposed to be acting all married to that woman? I can't risk you blowing this, Ethan, you can't call me and talk to me. What if someone finds out? What if you blow our chances for this money?" She was growing irritated with him, too, which after facing an angry Haley, was no picnic for him.

"Erica, wait! I just... I just need to talk to you. I need to see you. I miss you!" he told her plaintively.

She was adamant. "Ethan, I swear to God if you mess this up I'm not going to forgive you. I am not going to meet you! What if we get caught? You're willing to blow a hundred thousand dollars for a quick roll in the hay? Are you serious? If you get that horny, just screw the chick you're married to, but don't you dare blow that money! Now get off the phone and don't call me back!" she demanded angrily.

She hung up and he looked at the phone and sighed. "I love you, too, baby." he said in a low voice.

Joe and Harvey had shot it through the window, and both of them looked at each other and shook their heads.

Ethan laid in bed that night thinking that maybe, as much as he hated to admit it, Haley had a point. He had been slightly lackadaisical around the house. Haley laid in bed thinking what an idiot he was for having gotten them into the mess of having to sleep in the guest bedroom, but feeling a little bad for having yelled at him so much and thrown his wet shorts at him.

The next day they didn't speak to each other, and Ethan made a point of picking up his things around the house and making sure the kitchen sink wasn't full, but Haley didn't say anything to him because they were still going to be sleeping in the guest room one more night.

Two days later, they had a call from Valerie who told them she was sending the limo to pick them up and bring them in for a meeting with the producers. They dressed and rode silently in the car to the appointment.

When they walked into the meeting, they saw several familiar faces, most belonging to people they had either auditioned in front of or met at their wedding.

They were seated and Murphy looked at them seriously.

"Your show is doing really well, but there is a huge consensus that wants to see you two falling in love. Everyone adores you both but there is frustration that there are no sparks at all between you. We want you to change that. We want you to act like you're falling in love.

"The fight scene was great. Huge response from the viewers, but now they want a make-up between you both. You'll have to do that immediately," he told them in no uncertain terms.

Haley frowned. "You're telling us how to act around each other?"

Murphy looked at her and nodded solemnly. "I am. It's in your contract. Actors will adhere to the decisions that the administration deems necessary for the success of the show. In English, we tell you how to act around each other. We want you two to act like you're falling in love. It's all about the ratings. Always. Get going on it."

Ethan and Haley stared at him and then looked everywhere but at each other.

The meeting ended shortly after that and they were taken back to the house. They both were quiet but there was a gentler air between them, and as she walked through the kitchen and saw him loading the dishwasher, she realized that he was making an effort and she knew she had to commend that.

"Thank you for trying to pick up your end of things." she said quietly.

He shrugged. "No problem. I'm sorry I wasn't doing it before. I guess I just wasn't thinking about it," he told her.

It was quiet between them the rest of the day, but by the time they went to bed, their anger had gone and they laid close there in the dark of the guest bedroom. Harvey and Joe had finally left and they were free to talk honestly to one another.

"Are you asleep?" she asked him in a low whisper.

He sighed. "No. I can't sleep. You either?" he asked her in return.

"Not really, no. How do we act like we are falling in love with each other? I have had boyfriends but I haven't ever been in love with anyone before; you know... really in love. I don't know how that feels or what that's like. Do you?" she asked, turning her head toward him.

She could just make out his silhouette as he laid there looking at the ceiling. "Yeah. I... I was in love with an incredible girl, but some things happened and now we aren't together." He didn't think of it as a lie. He just didn't bother to mention that he was still in love with her and he would give anything to be with her just then.

"How do we act like we are in love?" she asked him. "What are they looking for?"

He sighed again and turned his head toward her. "I guess things like holding hands, hugging, probably kissing. Doing nice and thoughtful things for each other. You know... don't you? How have you never been in love before?" he asked in curious surprise.

"You're a really beautiful woman. I guess I'd have assumed that you would have been in love probably a couple of times by now. How come it hasn't happened?"

She looked away from him, back up at the ceiling. "I don't know. I guess I didn't think about it too much. I just haven't met anyone who makes me feel like they are my whole world. Isn't that what it's supposed to be like? Like they are your everything, you are their everything and there's nothing you wouldn't do for each other?"

He grinned. "That's it exactly."

Haley frowned. "How is love lost? I mean, if you loved someone and she loved you back just as much, how does either of you let it go?"

Ethan didn't quite know what to say to her. "I had to let her go. There were circumstances beyond my control that pulled me away from her. I didn't really have a choice in the matter. I'd have given almost anything to stay with her."

"She must have had such a hard time letting you go, too." Haley said with a soft sigh. "I'm sure she was just as devastated to lose you as you were to lose her."

The way Haley said it seemed to strike a light on a truth that Ethan had not really seen before. Erica had not been devastated to lose him. She had not had a hard time letting him go, and she did not seem to be having a hard time living without him. She was focused on the money. Maybe she was just anxious to hit the goal so that he could come back to her. He told himself that that was what it was, but somewhere, in the back of his mind, he didn't quite fully believe it.

"So I guess we start being more affectionate tomorrow," he told her quietly. He had to get the money. They couldn't fail at their endeavor. He had to find a way back to Erica, get the money, and then they could be together and be happy, and he could prove to her how much he loved her.

"Okay," sighed Haley. "I guess we will. Good night," she said in a quiet voice.

"Goodnight," he answered back. It was the first time they had said it to each other.

The next day they were both much more friendly to each other, speaking more pleasantly, and they felt like they were on the same team, trying to make it through the obstacle course of their marriage. Ethan even went out of his way to hold her hand once and kiss her on the cheek.

They were scheduled to meet each other's parents and neither one of them was looking forward to it. The car came and picked them up, and dressed beautifully, they went to into their parents' homes to introduce each other to their parents. Cameras rolling.

Haley's parents were first. Her parents welcomed him into their home, but her father was furious with her and her mother was nothing short of dumbfounded.

"Mama, Daddy, this is Ethan. Ethan, these are my parents, Isaac and Patricia."

"I've been watching you on television!" her mother told her, aghast. "What in the world are you doing? You didn't tell anyone about this, you didn't ask us anything, you didn't even invite us to your own wedding! You just ran off and got married! What were you thinking?" her mother asked her.

Her father wouldn't speak to either of them.

"Mama, I am just lucky that they picked me for this show. It's just to see if two strangers can fall in love, you know, like an arranged marriage. I thought I'd give it a try," she told her mother earnestly.

Her mother shook her head. "Well, I might not agree with it, but I am always going to be here for you, baby, and if this is something you think you want to try, then I'm going to support you. Your father is going to need some time."

That much was obvious to all of them. Ethan was well mannered and polite. He shook her mother's hand and extended his hand to Haley's father, but her father did not take it. He only looked seriously at Ethan.

"You treat my baby girl like she is the only thing keeping you alive on this planet," he told Ethan, and Ethan knew that as far as her father was concerned, the concept was true.

"Yes, sir, I will do that."
They left and once they were back in the car, they both heaved a great sigh and he looked out of the window as she rubbed her hands over her forehead.

"I'm so sorry that it went like that," she told him regretfully.

He shrugged. "I didn't expect much, I mean, this is a pretty strange situation. My parents aren't going to be any happier than yours are."

He was wrong. His mother was ecstatic.

"Haley, these are my parents, this is my mom, Louise Richards, and this is my dad, Warren. Mom, Dad, this is Haley, my... my wife." He hadn't meant to trip over saying it, but he recovered by hugging her shoulders as his parents reached to pull her into a hug.

"My son! My beautiful son is starring in this fantastic show and you are his beautiful bride! I never thought I'd have a daughter in law as exotic and gorgeous looking as you, although Erica was quite a good looking girl, too. Well, welcome to the family!" She bubbled as she kept grinning wildly at the cameras and fluttering all around the couple like a butterfly.

Ethan's father was quiet and shy, but welcoming. He smiled a lot and let his wife do all of the talking, which he couldn't have stopped her from doing anyway.

"It's so exciting, don't you think? Doesn't it feel exciting to you both?" Ethan's mother asked them with a grin.

They nodded numbly and smiled for the cameras, and Ethan took her hand. "It's quite a change for both of us. We are just learning to live together, though, you know. There's a little adjustment period, but I know that's true for anyone who moves in with someone else. She's very understanding and helpful and I think it's going really well."

Haley looked at him, grateful that he was being so kind to her on national television and in front of his parents.

They visited for a short while and then Harvey waved at them and they made their goodbyes and went back out to the car to go home.

"Thank you," Haley told Ethan with a smile. "You made that feel a lot easier than I thought it was going to be. I was so nervous."

"I was nervous too, but it worked out alright. It's all going to work out," he said, trying to convince them both, but he held her hand in his, even in the car where there wasn't anyone to watch them, and it felt like she had made a friend that she could rely on.

A few days later, she took down some of the pictures around the house and hung up some of her own decorations, photographs, and favorite pieces of famous works of art. She was surprised when, later that day, she walked through the living room and saw her framed works on the table and in the places where they had been hanging on the wall, she saw photographs of sportsmen, rock climbers, landscapes and rock bands that she had never seen before.

She looked at her pile of photos and artwork on the table and grew angry. She called for him and he came in from the kitchen.

"What?" he asked, walking in.

"Why did you take my things off of the wall?" she asked, looking at him with her hands on her hips. The cameras were rolling.

"You took up all the wall space all over the whole house," he told her with a frown. "I get some of the wall space, too. I'm just taking part of it. I didn't even take all of your things down, just some of them."

She narrowed her eyes at him. "Did you take them down in other rooms, too?"

His voice raised and he put his hands on his hips. "Yeah. So what?"

Haley grew angry with him. "I don't want you touching my things and moving them around! That's what! I put them all up where I wanted them and that was it, and now you've put up all this... this... junk... who is that? Maroon 5? On the wall? Can't you put that kind of crap up on the wall in your man cave or in the garage?"

Ethan was truly annoyed with her. "Just because you don't like it doesn't mean I can't put it up! We're sharing the house, we share the wall space! I don't care if you don't like it. If you don't like it, don't look at it!"

She was just about to lose her temper with him in a big way when she saw the red blinking light on the camera and she threw her hands up in the air in frustration and then covered her forehead for a moment, taking a deep breath.

"Okay, this is obviously going to be a problem for us, so we have to work it out. What if we do this -- you get certain walls and I get certain walls. We'll divvy it up. Okay? I don't want to fight with you again."

He lifted his chin and looked at her in annoyance. "Alright," he said, pointing to the wall they were standing beside. "I get this wall. Every one of them stays right where it is."

She glared at him. "I'm not keeping Maroon 5 on my living room wall! That's not decor... we aren't in high school or college. That kind of thing needs to be somewhere less... noticeable."

He shook his head and pointed at it. "I called it. It's my wall. If you want some walls, you better start claiming them right now."

She growled in frustration and grabbed her pictures, leaving him in the living room. She went to the front porch and sat on the swing, trying to keep the hot angry tears she felt stinging her eyes from falling down her cheeks. Haley picked up the phone and Joe and Harvey were nearby, camera rolling.

"Leslie!" she gasped into the phone, unable to hold her tears back when she heard her friend's voice. "I don't think I can do this! He's so difficult! I didn't know it would be this hard. I just don't think I can see this through all the way to the end of the season. I don't think it's worth the money, and I don't think it's worth the time. I'm so stressed out here!" she wept bitterly. "I can't stand it!"

What she didn't know was that Ethan was standing on the other side of the open window behind the porch swing, listening to everything she said.

He left before she finished her call, walking into the living room and looking at the pictures he had put up in place of hers. They looked fine to him, but as he considered it, he realized that his father's photos of sports heroes and historic things were all put up in his den, which at his parent's house, was his father's man cave. His mother didn't allow things like that out in the rest of the house. He realized it probably didn't look very fashionable to have them out in a main room of the house like that.

He thought about what she had had up, and sighed, realizing that she had put fine art pieces up in the living room. Works of art that even he knew on sight. He couldn't afford to lose this gig, not after everything they had already been through. He was sure that the hardest part was over, and that if they could just make it to spring, he would have the money that Erica wanted so badly. He would be able to take her to New York and she could follow her dream.

Ethan quietly took down all of his pictures and walked out to the man cave with them, setting them up in there, and relinquishing the living room to Haley. She had tried to work with him on it and be nice about it by suggesting that they each claim different walls, but he had been stubborn and now she was ready to quit and cost them both not only all of the money they were both trying to get, but also their public reputation, and the time they had already invested in making it happen.

Erica would never forgive him if he went back to her without the money, as a quitter of the show. He had to find a way to make it right, and he knew just how he was going to start making changes to keep them together, at least until the end of the season.

Chapter 5

Ethan went to the kitchen and began to cook a big meal. He cut vegetables and meat, he boiled and chopped and stirred and baked. He simmered and sautéed and all the while he was singing Christmas songs.

A short while later, Haley walked in and stopped in her tracks, looking at him.

"What are you doing?" she asked quietly.

He looked over his shoulder and smiled at her. "I'm cooking dinner for us. Something special. I was pretty thoughtless and selfish today and I want to make it up to you."

She couldn't help but smile back. Just the sight of him in the kitchen, his golden hair tied back in a ponytail as he moved about working with the food, occasionally wiping his fingers on the apron he was wearing, was enough to make her want to be happy.

She walked slowly toward him and began to peek in the bowls and dishes and poke around a little at the food to see what he was doing. "Did I hear you singing Christmas songs?" she asked him.

He shrugged. "Yeah, I love Christmas songs. It's my favorite time of year. I just love to see all that peace and kindness all over the place. Just about everyone feels it, the whole month long during December, and it's really wonderful. I wish we were all like that with each other every day and not just for a month once a year. Can you imagine? This world would be a different place."

She had to agree. "You're right about that," she said, laughing and shaking her head. "But it's still a little early for Christmas songs."

He walked toward her, his eyes on her, and he reached his arms around her and pulled her to him in a gentle embrace. "It's never too early for peace and kindness, or love and joy." He leaned forward and kissed her forehead, and the moment his lips touched her skin, she knew he was right. It was never too early for that at all.

Haley grinned up at him and he gazed at her happily for a moment and then let her go, returning to his bubbling, steaming kitchen.

She slipped her hands behind her and rested them on the back of her hips. "Well, is there anything I can help you with?" she offered sweetly.

He bit his lip and tilted his head. "I could use a taste tester," he told her and she went over to him. He held out a bite of some of the food he was cooking. She closed her mouth around it and then closed her eyes, savoring the bite. It was incredible. She wasn't expecting it to be so good, and unfortunately for her, that showed on her face.

Surprise overtook her and her eyes opened and grew wide and he looked mock-offended at her.

"You didn't think it was going to be good? Do you like it?" he asked, laughing at her.

She swallowed. "I loved it! I just didn't know it was going to be so delicious!"

Ethan threw his head back, laughed for a moment, and then looked at her with a shake of his head. "You thought it wasn't going to be that good! Well... how about that, missy? Good stuff, huh?" he asked with raised eyebrows.

"It's amazing!" She smiled at him, looking for another bite a moment later.

He shook his head. "You tried that one; now here's this... try this one." He gave her a bite from a pan with meat and vegetables in it.

She nodded and chewed, and when she swallowed, she told him how good it was and he looked totally triumphant.

"That's so great!" he said happily. "I'm so glad that you like my cooking."

"You should open a restaurant. You'd make a fortune!"

Joe and Harvey brought the cameras in closer and they were given bites as well, while filming. They nodded in agreement with Haley's suggestion about a restaurant. Harvey indicated that Ethan should kiss Haley and though it seemed awkward for them both, Ethan wrapped his arm around her and dipped his finger in a bit of chocolate in a bowl near him. He dabbed it on her lips when she wasn't paying attention and she stared at him in surprise.

He neared her and lowered his mouth to hers, sucking the chocolate off and kissing her, lightly at first, but as his lips and tongue moved over her mouth, she drew her breath in sharply and closed her eyes, losing herself in his kiss, in the moment, and she opened her mouth and kissed him back.

She caught him by surprise, and what had begun as a playful tease, heated to an intimate and sensual moment between them both. Haley felt as if everything around her was falling away except him; his strong arms holding her to his strong chest, his mouth taking her to breathless places she had never known before.

She felt her heart begin to pound and her belly tightened in warmth as his arms and hands closed firmly on her back, holding her to him, and somehow all of that together made her sigh softly.

The sound made Ethan pull back from her in an instant, blinking as if he was momentarily disoriented. The cameras rolled close, and Haley and

Ethan shared a hot and confused gaze for a lingering moment, their lips parted and swollen, their breath short and shallow, and then they blinked and looked away from each other.

"Why don't I go set the table," she told him over her shoulder.

"That would be helpful, thank you," he answered, becoming very interested in the pans and pots on the stove.

Joe and Harvey shared a quiet grin and kept filming.

A short while later, they were eating dinner together at the dining table, both of them anxious to talk about anything that took their minds off the awkward and steamy moment that they shared. They talked about their childhoods and how they grew up. They shared stories of being in school and jobs they had worked at, and found that they had a bit more in common than they ever would have guessed, and the feeling of friendship bloomed between them. The cameras got it all.

When it was time for bed, they said goodnight to Harvey and Joe, and then headed to their room. Ethan used the bathroom first and when Haley went into it, she saw that he had kept it clean for her, and she smiled in heartfelt appreciation. The terms her mother had used about training husbands came into her mind and made her chuckle to herself.

She went to their bed and climbed in, turning her back to him.

"Goodnight, Ethan." She smiled as she closed her eyes.

He was quiet a moment. "Haley..." he said quietly.

She opened her eyes and turned her head and then her body to face him. "Yes?"

He took a deep breath. "I just wanted to say that today was really fun and I think we did really well on the show. I think the producers are going to be happy with us..." he paused.

"I think so, too."

"But I just wanted to make sure that you knew that the uh... that the kiss tonight was just for the cameras. You know that, right? We're okay, you and me. We're friends?" He turned his head and looked at her.

He had been worried about it from the moment she had sighed in his arms, his tongue twisted with hers, his arms locked around her, his groin warm. He had been worried. He could not afford to have anything happen between them. Erica had told him to "'screw the woman he was with if he got horny," but he was sure she didn't mean it. He wouldn't cheat on Erica. He loved her and he couldn't wait to be back with her the moment his phony marriage was over.

He just had to make sure that the involuntary sigh that came from deep in Haley wasn't something that was going to become awkward for them.

"Oh yeah, of course. I know that. Are you expecting this marriage to last beyond the season?" she asked him point blank. She had been wondering about it, because she certainly didn't expect it to last, she had every intention of getting divorced, but he might not realize that and she didn't really want to lead him on; she liked him too much to do that.

He turned to look at her fully, his eyes wide and his voice quiet. "No, Haley, I'll be honest with you, I'm not. I hope that doesn't hurt you."

She smiled at him and shook her head. "Oh not at all... no, I'm not planning for it to last, either. This is just for the money for me."

Ethan breathed a great sigh of relief. "For me, too. I'm so glad you told me that. I felt so bad about ending everything when the season is over."

"Don't feel bad. We can be happily divorced friends. How about that?" she asked with a grin.

"That sounds like a dream come true! Goodnight, Haley."

"Goodnight Ethan," she replied, and that night they faced each other when they fell asleep.

Both of them fell asleep thinking about the kiss, as it played in their minds and lingered on their lips.

In the days that followed, they got along much better, and when the camera was on them, they smiled, laughed, and talked, and sometimes they kissed lightly, but they were careful not to kiss too closely, or hold each other too long and too near.

All the same, they felt a trust between them, born of the secret that they shared; the secret that they were going to let each other go at the end of the season. It made a base of friendship for them. It twinkled in their eyes when they looked at each other, because the whole nation was watching, and no one knew but them.

She was sitting in the kitchen a few days after their heated kiss. Sunlight streamed through the kitchen windows and lit the easel on which she was painting. She had pulled her paints and brushes out of a box she'd brought with her. She laid out some canvases in the well-lit breakfast nook and turned on some old jazz music from the thirties and forties.

Haley was painting away, trying not to dip her paintbrush in her coffee cup when Ethan walked in the back door, having come from the man cave. He stopped as he closed the door softly behind him, watching her. She was singing along to Ella Fitzgerald, moving her paintbrush along the canvas, red strokes pouring out behind the bristles of the brush.

She picked up another brush, and blue like the color of the midday sky high up above the earth was left in the wake of her brush. The song changed and she was singing Billie Holiday. He watched her quietly, entranced by what she was doing. He stood still for a long while, and he walked toward her a step at a time, until he was standing behind her.

He reached a hand out to her shoulder, knowing she was not aware of his presence. She jumped and gasped at his touch and her hand flew to her mouth as she turned and laughed at him.

"You startled me!" she said with a grin.

"I'm sorry, I just didn't want to disturb you, but I want you to tell me about what you're doing," he said, gazing into her eyes. Sea green, with flecks of dark green, blue, and gold in them, but mostly sea green, he decided, just as the sea would be on a sunny day, dancing in the wind. His gaze dropped to her lips for a moment; her soft sweet tasting lips.

He blinked and took a breath, looking at the painting behind her. "So, what are you painting?" he asked, looking at it in fascination.

"It's a sailboat on the ocean. It's late afternoon, so you can see these different colors in the water from the light. Light is so important," she told him as she showed him the different aspects of the work she was doing.

Ethan grinned. "I love it. This is wonderful work." He told her as he rested his hand on her back. She felt as if she was glowing inside. She was proud of her work, but she hadn't expected to hear that he liked it so much. She thought that he was more interested in sports and rock bands and not at all interested in anything much more than that. But he began to talk with her in depth about her painting as he stood beside her, so close to her, close enough that his chest was almost against her shoulder.

His hand on her back felt like an anchor holding her to him, making her feel an indescribable need to turn around and bury herself in his strong arms. She felt warm and serene beside him, like a cat would feel lying in the warm sunshine, and it took everything in her to focus on the painting instead of on the man who was almost intoxicating to her at her side.

"What are you going to do with this when you're done?" he asked her curiously.

She shrugged. "Put it with the rest of them, I guess."

He turned and looked at her in surprise. "The rest of them? How many do you have?"
"So many..." she sighed. "So many. I've been painting for a long time, though I haven't really had much time to paint over the last couple of years. I have time now, and I really wanted to get back into it. Then there's the question of what to do with them. I want to show them in a gallery and sell them, but I haven't

found any galleries who are willing to take them yet. It's hard to get them in and get started."

Ethan shook his head. "How could it be so hard?" he asked. "You have so much talent. This is a gorgeous picture."

She smiled. He was sweet, but he didn't have any real basis on which he could compare the true quality of her work; at least none that she knew about.

"Thanks, Ethan. I'm just going to keep painting them and who knows; maybe someday I can open my own art gallery." She took a deep breath and sat back down on her stool, picking up her paintbrush.

He looked around her then, at the small breakfast nook where she was painting. The table was covered in paint and brushes, cups of water, towels, paper towels, and other things.

"It doesn't look like you have much room to work in here," he told her quietly.

Haley looked around her and shrugged. "There isn't anywhere else in the house that I have this much light and space to work, so this is it. It's alright. It will do," she said quietly. "Unless you want to have breakfast in here..." She looked at him and laughed and he shook his head and reached for her, hugging her around the shoulders and kissing her forehead.

As he embraced her, she caught his scent, breathing him in as his chest neared her face and for a moment, she felt she had lost herself in the smell; the clean, comfortable, sweet, delicious smell of him that wrapped itself around her and held her just as close as his arms did.

She closed her eyes as his lips touched her forehead, and for a moment, she wished that he would keep holding her that way, but he let her go. She smiled up at him and he stepped back away from her.

"I'll let you get back to it." He walked to the door with a wave.

She nodded and turned back to her painting, picking up a paintbrush and reaching for her paint. He stood there by the door and watched her as she went back to her task, humming quietly and then forgetting he was there, her humming became singing again, and he found himself wanting to stay there in that moment for a long, long time.

Harvey and Joe traded smiles as they filmed it all, and they nodded their heads in approval.

Over the next few days, Haley almost never saw Ethan except when he was coming and going from his man cave. He smiled and hugged her as he came and left, he was there for dinner each night and they loved cooking together and loved the time they shared at night, but each day he was gone, all day, and she spent the free quiet time painting.

She didn't notice that the only time he paused in his comings and goings was to stop and watch her paint. The rest of the time, he was in and out of the house, though mostly out of it. He had boxes arriving regularly, and he carted the boxes out to his man cave and vanished for long periods of time. Harvey and Joe caught all of it.

They also captured all of the moments between the couple as their looks and smiles and touches lingered on each other, and the moments when their eyes stayed just a little longer on the other one when the other one wasn't looking.

One night after dinner, they were in the den looking for a movie to watch together. They were flipping through options on the television and discussing what kind of movie to watch when Ethan's phone rang and he picked it up and looked at it. His brows knit and he frowned slightly.

"Just a second, Haley. I'm sorry," he said, looking at the caller.

"Who is it?" she asked curiously.

He paused. "It's... ah... it's family. I'll be right back. Go ahead and pick out a movie for us. I'll be right back." He ducked out of the house and went to the man cave. Harvey and Joe followed him.

The door of the shed closed behind him, but not fully, and it was all too easy for Harvey and Joe to record his call.

"Erica! What's going on, baby? Are you alright?" he asked worriedly.

"Yeah, I'm great. I just keep watching this show and I'm wondering how things are going there," she said shortly.

"Things are good here. It's better than I thought it was going to be. It's easier. I thought it was going to be awful, but it really isn't," he told her quietly.

"Yeah, I can see that." she told him brusquely. "Listen, baby, don't get all wrapped up in that girl, okay? You are in this for the money. Just keep your eyes on the money." She sounded to him as if she was setting a mandate and he frowned.

"I'm not, Erica, don't worry about anything. We're just getting to know each other, that's all." He couldn't believe that he sounded defensive or that she felt like she had to even say anything like that to him. "I love you, baby, I'm doing this for you. You're the only reason I'm doing this." He said it with less honesty than he felt.

"Good. Just keep your eyes on that money. That's the only thing that matters. Not that chick. She's just the means to an end, Ethan; she is just the way to reach the money. Don't you forget it."

"Of course, baby, of course." He sighed. "I love-" but then he stopped. She had hung up on him.

He looked down at his phone and frowned, and then went back into the house, not noticing Harvey and Joe who had stepped behind the big tree that grew beside the shed. They headed back to the house and had the camera rolling just in time to see Ethan walking to the sofa in the den where Haley was waiting for him.

She grinned up at him. "I saved you a spot!" She patted the couch next to her. He nodded distractedly and went to sit beside her.

When he had sunk down into the cushions beside her, he wrapped his arm around her shoulders and she snuggled in to him, happy to rest her head on his shoulder as the movie started.

Before it was halfway over, he realized she had fallen asleep and he turned to look at her. She was so sweet and serene lying there in his arms, like a sleeping angel. He stared at her face; tracing his finger over her high cheekbones, her strong jaw line, the soft curve of her luscious lips. He marveled at her beauty and drew in a slow breath before leaning in and pressing his lips carefully and gently to her forehead.

His kiss lingered there for a long while. Then he looked down at her, feeling everything in him drawn to her, thinking of her laugh, her smile, the depth of her sea green eyes and her wide, wide open heart, and he leaned down and kissed her mouth tenderly. His lips brushed hers, and he closed his eyes, staying lightly for a moment, but then as he felt a warmth growing through him, he lifted his hand to her cheek, holding her face delicately as his kiss pressed in a little more.

Haley was dreaming of him, and in her dream he kissed her, and then she realized that she wasn't dreaming, but the dream was so delicious that she let herself be taken in by the warmth and she began to kiss him back, parting her lips and tasting him a little. He was startled that she had awoken, but as her tongue moved over his, it made him thirst for more of her, and his arms encircled her, cradling her closely and kissing her deeply.

Haley slid her arms around his neck and held him to her as her body began to heat up and respond to him. She grew breathless as they lost themselves in the moment and their tender kissing became sensual.

His hand moved from her waist up the side of her body and she felt his thumb glide over the side of her breast before he moved his hand to her back. It made her ache for him to touch her in ways that lovers touch.

Ethan felt his groin tighten with need and his heart quickened. He knew he had no business doing anything like this with her, especially if his beautiful Erica was going to be watching them. He slowly lifted his mouth from hers, his breath short and his eyes heavy with desire. He closed them and leaned his forehead against hers. She closed her eyes and let her hands close around the back of his neck for a moment.

She had to remind herself that this was a job, it was not real, that it was only for the camera that was rolling on them. Harvey and Joe had become such a constancy in their lives and so-called marriage that they hardly even noticed when their camera crew was around anymore. She knew they were there, though, quietly filming from the corner, and she drew a deep breath and let her arms fall away from Ethan who wasn't entirely sure he wanted to let her go at all.

Haley leaned back against the sofa. "It's late. We should call it a night."

He blinked and leaned back from her, trying to slow his heart and the blood that burned through him, making him hard for her. "Right. It is late. I have a lot to do tomorrow." He stood up from the sofa and then turned to hold out a hand to her to help her up.

"Do you?" she said offhandedly, trying to change the subject as she took his hand and stood up. "I noticed you've been out there a lot. What are you so busy with out there?" she asked interestedly.

He gave her a smile and shrugged. "Oh you know, just man cave stuff. Nothing exciting," he said as they headed to their room and readied for bed. Harvey and Joe didn't leave until the lights were off and both

Ethan and Haley were sleeping, both of them grinning at one another as they locked the door and closed it behind them.

Haley fell asleep thinking about Ethan's unexpected kiss. She wondered if he kissed her because of the cameras, because they were told to spice up their marriage for the nation and the show, or if he kissed her for some other reason, because it felt to her like he meant it. It felt to her like his arms around her and his mouth on hers was exactly where and how he wanted to be with her, and she had to admit to herself, finally, that it was exactly where she wanted him.

She didn't know if she was falling for him or if she was just curious, because they spent so much time around each other, and there weren't any other options, but she could not deny that there were feelings growing in her for him that seemed very real to her.

Ethan's dream and heart were a tangle of confusion as he fell asleep. Part of him was aching and reaching for Erica, and another part of him, part of that he didn't want to think about, or face, or even admit to, was longing for Haley. The warmth of her body beside him in the bed made his heart beat faster, made his arms ache to hold her, made his body want to feel her against him, made his skin bead up with perspiration as he struggled with facing the wall and telling himself that nothing mattered except the money. Nothing mattered except Erica and the money.

Chapter6

Two days later, early in the afternoon, Haley was painting another picture when Ethan walked into the kitchen quietly. He'd taken to tiptoeing in so that she wouldn't know he was there and he could watch her work for long moments without interrupting or distracting her, and she would continue in her sweet way, singing and painting.

Sometimes, if she was standing while she painted, she would sway a little, dancing just a bit as she painted, and she was completely happy in her element. He loved to see her like that, to watch her as she let all the wonderful creative beauty in her shine out of her like rays of sunshine and joy. He had never known anyone like that and it was fascinating to him.

He had admitted to himself at one point that he was addicted to seeing her like that; to standing in the distance where she couldn't see him, quietly watching her as she worked happily, making incredible artwork out of blank white canvases, coloring them with the endless wonders that were alive in her.

He let her paint and sing until she paused and set her brush down, stepping back to look critically at her picture. Then he walked toward her, and the closer he got to her, the more he felt like she was the sun at the center of his solar system, and all he wanted to do was close himself around her.

Ethan reached his hands out to her shoulders and she turned and looked over her shoulder at him as he pulled her back against him, her shoulders touching the muscled wall of his chest.

"What do you think of it?" she asked, looking back at the painting and closing her eyes, letting herself enjoy the feel of his body against hers for a moment.

"I love it. I love everything about it," he said seriously. "You're amazing. I think there's just one thing that needs to be changed, though."

She felt his deep voice in his chest, the vibration of it near her head, her ears, and she wished she could snuggle into him. She opened her eyes suddenly.

"What is it missing?" she asked with a hint of worry. She looked at it carefully. It looked like it ought to, she thought, but she knew she was looking at it with a subjective eye.

He smiled a little and she turned to see a twinkle in his eyes. He held out his hand to her. "Come with me. I'll show you just what's missing."

She lowered one eyebrow doubtfully, but put her hand in his and walked with him as he led her outside. Harvey and Joe were right behind them, as always, camera rolling.

He walked her to the man cave shed and she looked at it in surprise as she saw big new windows all the way around it from about four feet off the ground up to the roof, where the tiles that had once been there were replaced with a glass ceiling, like a greenhouse would have. He reached for the door handle and opened it up.

She walked inside and looked around in astonishment. There was a long counter set up with a deep double-sided sink, an array of shelves, and a small refrigerator along one wall. There was even a small coffee maker and a teapot and teacups set up on the counter, with an assortment of teas and coffees.

On the short wall at the far end of the room was a comfortable looking sofa for two, and the rest of the room was set up to be an art studio, with areas for easels, paints, shelves, and a table on one wall.

She looked around the area in disbelief. "How... What did...? What is this?" she asked incredulously, tripping over her words.

"It's your new art studio." He glanced at her with a shy smile, his hazel eyes shining as he watched her looking at him.

"My... what? You did this... you did all of this for me?" she asked in wonder. Haley couldn't believe it. She stared at him and then turned to look at it all again. Her second look around saw the cool old pottery coffee mugs hanging on a mug tree on the counter. There were fresh flowers in vases set around the room, and some of her pictures standing against the wall.

A cozy blanket and soft little pillows were on the sofa, and a radio set up near the drawing table. There were plants on little shelves all over the room, and a couple of hooks for sweaters near the door. There was even a little welcome mat inside the door.

She couldn't believe what she was looking at. He had taken his precious man cave and turned it into a wonderful little studio for her. Her hands flew to her mouth, covering it as she tried to hold in her emotion, but she turned to face him as he grinned at her, his hair falling loose over his face and his shoulder as he lowered his head a little.

Haley threw her arms around his neck and hugged him tightly, squealing in excitement.

"I can't believe you did this! It's incredible!" She laughed and he reached his arms around her and held her, closing his eyes and drawing her against him.

"You needed somewhere to work. You needed a place where creativity and inspiration could find you and the breakfast nook was just not the right place."

She felt tears springing to her eyes and wiped them away as she leaned back and looked up into his face. "This is the sweetest thing anyone has ever done for me. No one has ever given me anything like this. I can't believe it! What are you going to do for a man cave?" She wiped another tear from her cheek in complete happiness.

He shrugged. "I'll build another one right next to your studio. We have room right over there in the yard, so I can bring in another shed and make a man cave. Not so many windows, though, caves should be a little more secretive." He winked at her and she hugged him tightly again.

"Thank you, thank you so much," she said from her heart as she held him tightly. He rocked her slowly in his arms and kissed the top of her head, and then waited for her to let go first.

When she did, she turned and looked at her new studio as if it was a playground and she was a child. She went to each place in it, looking at everything he had placed so thoughtfully and carefully around, smelling the flowers, touching the sofa, playing with the radio.

"Would you like some tea?" she asked excitedly.

He nodded. "Sure! I'd love to help you break in your studio," he told her with a smile.

Harvey and Joe were grinning like idiots as they filmed the whole thing, and she made tea and coffee for everyone. Ethan and Haley were very good about taking care of the camera crew who was working so hard on their show, and Harvey and Joe appreciated it.

Ethan and Haley sat together on the sofa in her new place, enjoying it and each other, until it was eventually time for dinner, and then they cooked together and ate.

At bedtime, they said goodbye to the camera crew and readied to go to sleep. Haley was still amazed at the generosity and kindness that Ethan had showed to her. She had been reeling with bliss all day long, her grin not seeming to be able to leave her face.

She pulled on her soft tank top and silk shorts, brushed her teeth and went to bed. She crawled in beside her husband and laid there quietly, but she just couldn't get every single thought about the studio out of her mind. She had to thank him once more, just to tell him how grateful she was.

"Ethan..." she whispered, uncertain if he was awake.

He was lying there, playing the afternoon over and over in his head; her sheer delight and joy, her enthusiasm for the work he had done for her, her plans for all of the art that she was going to create in the studio, the feel of her in his arms when she held him to thank him.

He had wanted to kiss her, to share all the joy of the moment with her that way, but he had been struggling with his growing desire for her and he was nervous about that showing up for the camera, because he did not want anyone else to see how he was really feeling. Instead, he had just kissed the top of her head and denied himself what he wished he could have done.

"Yeah?" he asked quietly, turning over to look at her. She was so beautiful, lying there in the dim light from the muted glow coming in from the garden lights outside.

She grinned at him and took his hand in hers.

"You gave me the greatest gift ever today, and I just wanted to thank you once more, to tell you how much it really means to me. I have never had that kind of encouragement and support, or care about what I do, from anyone before.

"It was a little overwhelming at first when you showed me, and I just wanted you to know that it means everything to me, to my future, to my work. Thank you so much," she said in a hushed voice.

She leaned forward and kissed him softly on the mouth, intending for it to be a kiss of gratitude. But as her lips left his and she began to lean back, she paused, looking at him as he stared at her with some unreadable haunted look on his face; a look she had not seen before. It felt as if he needed her.

She leaned back to him and kissed him once more, just the merest brush of a touch of her lips against his at first, but then she pressed her lips more firmly against his, and her kiss became tender and sweet as her hand moved to touch his cheek and slip beneath his hair, pushing it back behind his head.

He could not hold himself back from her or resist her. The feel of her lips on his awoke a heat in him that he had been trying to ignore, but was no longer able to. He leaned into her kiss, parting her lips with his and running his tongue over hers. She responded immediately to him, tasting him back, and her arm moving behind his neck as she kissed him deeply.

Ethan let all of his reasons and excuses and inhibitions burn away in the growing flames of desire that began to take over every part of him. He rolled her onto her back and held himself above her, his mouth moving with hers, his hand moving from her waist down her bare leg to her knee. His fingers slid beneath her shorts and slowly he drew them upward, pulling them aside slightly and resting his body against her core.

Everything in her spiraled out of control and she became breathless as she felt him against her, hard and hot. He wasn't wearing anything but boxer shorts, and they did nothing to hide his growing desire for her.

She had never thought that they would ever be in a situation like they were, but she didn't want it to stop and she knew that he didn't, either. Haley ran her hands down over the muscles in his back from his shoulder to his hips, and when she reached them, she slid her fingers beneath the band of his boxers and squeezed him, pulling his hips tight against hers as she moved her body against his.

A muffled groan escaped him and he pressed himself harder against her, moving his hand up under her tank top, over her ribs to her full breast, cupping his hand around it, massaging it and running his fingertips over her hard nipple. She drew her breath in as she kissed him, immersing herself in the burning need for him that had taken over every one of her senses.

Their mouths and bodies moved against one another, building up the bonfires of need in them. He slid his hand from her breast down over her belly and into her shorts and panties, moving his fingers over the soft moist folds of her core. She gasped loudly and he gently slid his fingertips into her, drawing heat to them and making her writhe against him, succumbing to the pleasure he gave her.

She raked her fingers through his hair, curled her fingertips into it and clenched them, twisting and pulling gently as she arched her back and pushed her head back into the pillow as his lips and tongue traveled down her throat.

He leaned up and looked at her through heavily lidded eyes, his breath coming short and his voice hoarse.

"Haley...God, I need you so much. Make love with me... please..." he asked from his heart.

She opened her eyes and looked at him with a wide smile, leaning up to kiss his mouth. "Yes," she told him happily, "I want you, too."

He told himself that once, just this once, they could do this. After all, Erica had told him to, and he had never needed a woman the way that he needed Haley. It was as if everything about her had drawn him in and there was no part of him that was not saturated with her light, her beauty, her sweetness, and her love, He had never wanted to lose himself in a woman more. But as he pulled her clothes from her, spread her legs apart and gently pushed himself into her body, he discovered that he was finding himself in the way she held him so close, the way she wrapped her body around him and moved with him, her tender and sensual kisses. She took her time loving him, giving him back every single bit of attention, love, and affection that he gave to her.

She felt him filling her, moving in and out of her, sending waves of pleasure rushing through her whole body as they rocked against one another, holding each other close, tossing and turning in their bed, clinging to each other tightly as passion overflowed in them like a raging river that could not be tamed.

Their tempest built itself up, harder and stronger until both of them were lost to it, crying out in release and ecstasy, arms locked in love around each other as their bodies trembled and tightened, then finally relaxed into sated bliss.

It was long moments before they finally let each other go, each one alone and breathing more slowly, astounded at the experience they had shared.

She turned her head and looked at him. "Now what do we do?" she asked, wondering where in the world this left them both.

He looked at her and reached for her. "You come to me and sleep in my arms where I have wanted you to be for a while, and we dream together," he whispered, folding her into his warm and gentle embrace.

They had not bothered to close the bedroom door that night and when the camera crew came in the next morning, they shot a little footage from the doorway and the foot of the bed as the couple slept wrapped up in each other, and barely wrapped up in a sheet. Then Harvey and Joe closed the door and waited for them out in the kitchen.

Ethan woke up to the smell of coffee and Haley laying in his arms. He stared at her, resting there against him peacefully, her wavy hair spilled around her like a dark halo. He didn't regret anything they had done, but he did wonder what would happen, what would change for them now that they had made love.

He never realized before how very different having sex and making love were. All the times he had been with Erica, he had believed without question that it was love, but wrapped up in Haley's body, in her tender and sweet embrace after a night of real love, he found he could not compare it with any other intimacy in his life. He became aware that what he had shared with Erica was sex. Amazing, hot, rock star sex, but nothing more than sex, all the same.

What he and Haley had experienced in one another's arms was much more than that. It was hot, no question, but it was also beautiful and it seemed precious. It felt like it was something he could never tire of wanting, or ever want to lose.

What he had shared with Haley had put his previous affairs into such sharp relief that his experiences in bed with Erica felt dirty, in a way; a way that made him not want to go back to them. His eyes moved from Haley's face and traveled down over her body, partially covered in the sheet.

He lifted it from her carefully and his gazed drifted ever so slowly over her rounded breasts, her narrow waist and the curve of her hips. His eyes moved to the triangle of curls between her thighs. It wasn't more than a few moments later that his fingers were touching her there, caressing her as she woke up and her eyes opened to him.

She smiled and moaned softly, stretching and sliding her legs open to give him more room. His mouth covered her breasts and nipples as he took his time arousing her, and before long, he was thrusting himself into her again, holding her tightly against him and making love with her in the bright morning light.

They loved just as passionately as they had the night before, and when they climaxed, they held on to each other tightly, and for a long while afterward, when the bliss had evolved into peace. They showered together and dressed for the day.

"I think the guys made coffee," she said as she pulled her clothes on.

He smiled. "I think they made it a while ago. I think they've been waiting for us."

The two of them went out into the kitchen and found Harvey and Joe sitting at the breakfast bar on the island, grinning behind their coffee cups.

"Morning, guys." Ethan smiled at them.

"We made honeymoon waffles. They're in the toaster," Joe said with a wink.

Harvey elbowed him and cleared his throat. "Murphy is sending a car for a meeting with you two in a bit. You probably have half an hour."

Haley raised her eyebrows. "Really? Well that gives us just enough time to eat Joe's honeymoon waffles and some fruit before we have to go." She winked at them and Joe blushed.

Half an hour later, they were on their way to the office.

Murphy sat them both down and told them that things were going well, and then he sat alone with Haley and talked to her earnestly.

"I have seen some changes happening between you both, but it's happening too slowly. I need you to show more affection for him. You really need to look like you're falling in love with him. Pour it on. Make it real. Make it believable," he told her.

Thoughts of the passionate love-making the night before and that very morning flooded her mind and she felt heat rising to her cheeks as she smiled at Murphy. "I don't think that's going to be a problem," she told him with a smile.

"I mean it, Haley. You have to look like you are falling head over heels for your husband. Make the whole nation believe it. I'll put it this way. There isn't any length you could go to that would be too far. Things between the two of you need to be a lot hotter. Do you understand what I'm saying?" He looked at her meaningfully.

She lowered one brow at him for a moment as she comprehended what it was he was really saying. He was telling her that he wanted her to get physical with Ethan and make it obvious to the cameras and the world. He didn't know that they had made love already. That was still a secret. She realized that he had no idea things had changed as they had between her and Ethan, and what he was telling her to do was something he expected of her without objection, in essence, telling her to have sex with Ethan for the sake of the show, not for any romantic reason.

"I'll give it some thought, Murphy." she told him with a stoic face.

He shook his head at her. "I don't want thought. I want skin. I want heat. I want ratings, and that's what the public wants to see. That's what needs to happen."

She hated that he was so willing to sell her to the masses for profit. "I'll see what I can do to make that happen," she told him quietly. There was no use in arguing, they had already made love twice, and things between them were going to be obvious to the public eye very soon.

"Good. One other thing; you are no longer allowed contact with anyone outside of the house, and the show has been restricted from showing in your home. You won't be able to see it for a while," he told her matter-of-factly.

She was stunned. "I can't call my parents or even Leslie? Why not? Why is the show banned?" she asked, her anger growing deeper.

He didn't even blink. "I want you to focus on Ethan, and I don't want you to be distracted by... outside influences. Except for business, no outside contact for you," he told her in a stony voice.

Haley glared at him. "You can't keep me from talking to anyone!"

He leaned forward and rested his arms on the desk, leveling his gaze at her. "I can do anything I want to; it's in your contract."

She was fuming, angry with him, but she could see that she wasn't going to get anywhere with it. She stood up and walked to the door, yanking it open.

"Send Ethan in, please." He leaned back in his chair.

She walked out of Murphy's office in fury and Ethan gave her a concerned look.

"What's wrong?" he asked, his hands holding her shoulders as he looked at her.

"Nothing. Don't worry about it. He wants to see you."

Ethan sighed and kissed her forehead, and then walked into Murphy's office, closed the door and sat before his desk.

Murphy stood up out of his chair and walked over to the front of his desk, leaning against it and looking down at Ethan.

"Ratings have been falling for the show, and we need to work fast to get them back up again," he said resolutely. "I have an extra little bit of of camera work for you to do, although, this could hardly be called work." Murphy chuckled deeply.

Ethan looked at him. "What is it?" he asked curiously.

Murphy watched him like a hawk. "I want you to go downstairs to an office we have set aside for visits. A guest down there wants to see you. I think you'll be... *excited*... to see her," he said with emphasis.

Ethan frowned. "Who is it?"

He laughed lasciviously for a moment. "Erica, your girlfriend."

Ethan knew that it was useless to argue that he didn't have a girlfriend, though it was the first thought that crossed his mind. "What... how did you know..." he tried to ask as panic rushed through him.

Murphy just smiled. "We are recording everything, Ethan. You've had phone calls from her, and we did background research on both of you. We knew about her before I called you. Now, go downstairs and spend some time with your hot girlfriend. I'm sure you miss her. I know I would. Go... let off a little steam before you go home with Haley."

Ethan felt a strange mixture of the thrill of seeing Erica, and the dread of it; he'd spent incredible time with Haley, and he knew that Erica had told him to do it, but he felt like he was betraying them both in a weird way.

"I don't think it would be good for the show, Murphy." Ethan was not sure what to do.

Murphy just laughed at him. "It's okay; it's just this one time. Just to boost the ratings. The fans will love it. Just... go get some action in before you leave. I want you to steam up the camera lens, you got me, Ethan? Go do to that woman what any red blooded man would want to do to her. You're a lucky son of a bitch, Ethan. So, go get lucky."

Murphy punched a button on his phone. "He's ready."

There was a knock at the door and Jason opened it and jerked his head at Ethan. Ethan felt his heart began to pound. He was going to see Erica. He couldn't deny that he was anxious to see her, that he had missed her horribly, but he was torn, particularly when he walked past Haley in the waiting room and she looked at him in surprise, as he told her he would be back in a while.

The receptionist at the desk waved and grinned at him as he walked out of the door. Jason took him down one floor and led him to a door that looked like every other door on the floor. When he opened it, Ethan walked in and found himself in what looked like a reception room; there were two sofas and four chairs arranged around a glass table.

Standing in the corner of the room was his own camera crew; Harvey and Joe, camera rolling, both of them looking away from Ethan as he walked in. Sitting on the couch was Erica. She smiled widely when he walked in, and she stood up. She was wearing a tight little black miniskirt, black stiletto heels, a black satin bra and a white button up blouse that wasn't buttoned up at all and was tied in a knot just beneath her barely covered breasts. Her wavy red hair was hanging down all around her, spilling over her back and her shoulders.

He felt his heart skip a beat when he saw her, and she strutted toward him with a sexy smile on her red lips.

"Hey baby... it's been a while," she said in a velvety voice.

He rushed to her and wrapped his arms around her, holding her tightly to him. "I missed you! I missed you so much."

"I missed you too, babe." She leaned back and looked up at him, sliding her arms around his neck and lifting her mouth to his. She kissed him hard and slid her hands slowly from his neck to his chest.

In her kiss, he felt the fire he was so used to with her; a rush of lust that always came when she was with him. It shot through him as she twisted her tongue around his, and raked her long nails over his chest, reaching them to his buttons and unbuttoning his shirt rapidly all the way to his waist.

"Come here, baby..." she told him seductively as she took his hand and led him to the long sofa. She pushed him down onto it with some force and then slowly slid her bare legs over his as she straddled him and flipped her hair to one side; the side away from the camera, giving the camera lens the perfect shot of her as she took over Ethan's mouth and drew his hands to her breasts.

He kissed her back, and an old hunger stirred deep in him as she worked her fingertips swiftly over the buttons on her own shirt. She pulled it off and tossed it to the floor, leaving only her strapless bra on.

Ethan felt his groin harden and she laughed deeply as she took his face in her hands and pulled it to her breasts, where he kissed the tops of them as he held her tightly.

"That's it, baby, get hard for me... get real hard." she told him. "Love me, baby...." she said in a throaty voice as she drew his hands up her thighs toward the hem of her micro miniskirt.

The word entered Ethan's mind and somehow, like a wrench in a machine, it suddenly stopped everything he was thinking. "'Love me" she had said, reaching for his erection and stroking it over his pants. He wasn't loving her, he was doing what he always did with her, which he had once believed was love, but which he had discovered was not love at all. It was lust. It was hot sex, but it was not love. His heart felt like it was going cold.

157

He pulled away from her and leaned back, looking at her with a strange expression on his face.

"I... I can't do this. I have to go," he said quietly. He put his hands on her waist and moved her off him, standing up a moment later.

Erica stared at him with a dropped jaw for a moment as he buttoned his shirt back up, and she stood up beside him, reaching for him and turning him to face her fully.

Her eyes flashed green fire at him and she curled her lip back slightly. "You are mine, baby, don't you forget that. You are just doing this for the money. Don't get all wrapped up in that little bitch you're living with right now. You are mine, and the money is mine, and I want you to remember that, baby. You keep your eyes on the money, and your mind on me."

She grabbed him and kissed him hard, running her hand over his crotch again. "This is mine," she said. He just looked at her and nodded stiffly, wiping her lipstick from his mouth and then turned to walk out of the door.

His heart felt like it was being torn in two. He was completely confused, and felt guilt both ways about it. She was right, of course, he was her boyfriend. It was her idea that he do this job, that he get the money, and that he give it all to her. The problem was that there was nothing in that for him, and at the beginning he was fine with that, because doing it for her to please her was enough for him, but things had changed a little bit.

He had made love with Haley, twice, and it had finally felt like there was something for him, other than just hot sex. He'd felt loved in return, and that was a revelation for him; one he wasn't sure he wanted to give up.

The camera crew walked out of the room and his eyes finally met theirs. They just watched him and then walked away silently.

Neither Haley nor he talked in the car on the way back to the house, but when they arrived there, the camera crew arrived a few minutes later.

Ethan felt bad the whole way home, but walking into their home with his wife made him feel like it could be alright again, so he turned on some of the music he knew she loved, and old jazz floated through the kitchen as he pulled all kinds of food from the refrigerator and started making dinner.

Haley walked into the kitchen and smiled when she saw what he was doing.

"Look at you, cooking for me again." she grinned, and he walked up to her and took her in his arms, slow dancing with her in the kitchen.

She laughed at him and danced along with him, enjoying it richly. "What brought this on?" she asked him curiously.

He looked at her in mock offense. "What, I can't dance with my wife if I want to?" he raised one eyebrow and dipped her, lifting her back up and kissing her tenderly as she stood back up.

She might have been angry with Murphy, and silent on the way home, but Ethan's lighthearted dance and warm kisses washed away everything she had been angry about, and all that was left was joy.

Haley closed her eyes and let her head fall back a little as his lips moved down her neck to her collarbone, but then she remembered the food and she gave him a little push.

"You're going to burn dinner!" she said with a half giggle and a slightly worried tone.

He spoke against her neck as he kissed her, muffling his reply. "I don't care. I'd burn down the house just to be able to be in your arms."

She laughed in earnest then and gave him another push, and he finally relented and let her go, walking dejectedly back to the stove to cook. She poured wine for them both and they sipped and talked and cooked together until dinner was done, and then they ate in the dining room and made sure to save two plates for Harvey and Joe in the kitchen.

When dinner was finished, Ethan looked at Harvey and Joe and smiled.

"I'm going to bid you two fine gentleman goodnight; I'm taking my wife to bed." he told them shamelessly.

They grinned and nodded, turning their cameras off and waving as Ethan and Haley vanished into their bedroom and closed the door behind them. He took his time taking her clothes off her, savoring every inch of her body, touching her delicately and tenderly, kissing her almost from head to toe before he couldn't hold himself back anymore, and he made love with her for a long while before they fell asleep in each other's arms.

Haley drifted off into her dreams in ecstasy, thinking how incredible it was that when she met Ethan on their wedding day, the only thing she could think of was how soon they could get divorced, but as she fell asleep in his arms, she knew that the last thing she wanted to do was be without him.

Chapter 7

A few days later, Haley was sitting in her studio, her music playing softly in the background as Louis Armstrong crooned away, the steam on her black coffee swirling upward, and the sun shining in on her as she drew her brush across the canvas.

Her phone rang and she bit her lip and looked at it. She was under strict orders from the network not to have any calls that weren't business calls, but she didn't recognize the phone number, so she answered it, hoping it was no one she knew personally.

"This is Haley." She said it almost hesitantly.

The voice that came through was a man's; deep and rich, pleasant and friendly. He spoke with what seemed like a Spanish accent. "Good afternoon, Haley. My name is Enrique Aragon. I am an art dealer. I own an art gallery in Los Angeles, and another in New York. I have seen some of your art on the television show that you are on, but I would like to come to your home to see it in person, if I may. I am interested in showing it in both of my galleries, if you are open to the idea."

He could have knocked her over with a feather if he was standing beside her, rather than talking with her on the phone. She was completely stunned for a moment, but somehow her brain began to function again and her lungs drew in a sharp breath, and she blinked and shook her head after a long moment.

"Mr. Aragon! My goodness..." she paused as she tried to think of what to say.

"Please, call me Enrique. May I please call you Haley?" he asked her.

She laughed lightly and held the phone close. "Yes, of course. Please do. I... I am just so excited. I never imagined I would get a call like this!" she tried not to gush, but it was almost impossible for her, given her state of unexpected delight.

He chuckled. "Well, being on television does give you a lot more exposure," he told her quietly.

She began to pace back and forth in her studio, paying no attention at all to Harvey and Joe who were filming her from the open doorway.

"Well, Mr. ...uh, Enrique, when would you like to come by the house? I'm here most of the time. I'd be glad to show you all the art I have, and if you are looking for anything in particular, I'm sure I could probably create it for you. I'm really versatile in my style and my mediums."

"That's excellent to hear, Haley. Why don't I come by next Wednesday afternoon? Say, four o'clock perhaps?" he asked with a congenial tone.

Haley grinned. "That's perfect, that would work really well for me. I'm actually just about finished with a piece that I could have ready for you by then, so it will be unseen by anyone else."

"I'm looking forward to it, and most especially to meeting you. It is rare to find someone with so much talent and beauty combined. I'll see you next Wednesday," he told her.

She felt heat rising to her cheeks as her heartbeat sped up. "Thank you, goodbye, Enrique," she said happily, trying to remain calm.

She hung up the phone and squealed loudly, clapping her hands over her face and then grinning at Harvey and Joe.

"Did you hear that? A gallery owner! Coming here to see my art! I can't believe it! Finally, someone who wants to sell my work. It's amazing and incredible!" she squeezed past them both and practically ran to the house.

Harvey looked at Joe. "You got all that?" Joe nodded and they followed her into the house.

"Ethan!" she called out. "Ethan! You'll never guess what just happened!"

He came out of the den, which had become his pseudo man cave, and looked at her in surprise.

"What? What just happened?" he asked curiously.

"I got a call from an art dealer! He owns a couple of galleries; one here and one in New York and he wants to come here to the house to see my work! I'm so excited! He says he wants to show it in the galleries! Isn't that exciting?" she asked gleefully.

He picked her up and hugged her tightly, squeezing her to him. "That's tremendous! I'm so glad for you!" he said as he kissed her sweetly and looked at her again, setting her down. "You work so hard, you deserve this. It's such a big change for you! I'm so proud of you," he told her with a big smile.

She grinned back and took his hands in hers. "Will you help me get ready for his visit? I am so nervous! I'm not sure what I should put out for him to see, or where... or..." her eyes grew wide with panic when the realization struck her that there would be an art dealer in her home looking at her artwork in just a few days' time.

Ethan chuckled and took her by the shoulders, looking into her eyes. "I will help you get it all set up. The house will look great, and you will impress him; that I promise you."

Ethan could not have been more right. Over the days leading up to Enrique's visit, they deep cleaned the house, gathered all of her works and hung them on several walls throughout their home and put her partially finished works up in her studio for him to see there.

On the day that he was to arrive, she put on a white sundress with spaghetti straps, a sweetheart neckline, a tapered waist and a flared skirt. She slipped some earrings in and pulled her wavy curls up on top of her head, cascading slightly down the back of her neck.

Ethan took one look at her and let out a long low whistle. "Wow, Haley, you look incredible." He grinned at her as she straightened her already straightened skirt.

"Don't worry, you look beautiful, the house looks beautiful, the artwork is hung and it looks beautiful... it's going to go so well. Just take a deep breath and tell yourself that it will be a fun and successful afternoon," he told her, holding her hands in his.

She closed her eyes. "It's going to be a fun and successful afternoon, " she repeated. She opened her eyes. "I'm still too nervous to even breathe."

He nodded his head. "Okay. I can fix this. Come with me." He led her to the kitchen where he pulled out a couple of bottles of wine and poured her a glass of one of them.

"Drinking wine while looking at art is practically expected. It's part of the whole art culture now, isn't it? Drink this," he said, handing the glass to her.

She sipped. She gulped. She emptied the glass. "No good. Still nervous." she said with a fretful look.

He chuckled. "It's okay. Here, have another one. You'll be alright, and I'll be right here with you to help you through it."

Harvey lowered his phone from his ear and looked at Ethan. "I'm afraid you won't, Ethan. This is Murphy on the line. He said he needs to meet with you right away. He's sending a car."

Haley's eyes grew wide and Ethan frowned. "Can it wait? This is a really important afternoon for her."

Harvey lifted the phone back to his ear and shook his head. "Nope. Murphy said it's urgent. The car is already on the way."

Ethan looked at Haley, taking her face in his hands and kissing her softly. "You are going to be wonderful. Just sip your wine and relax. It's all going to be just fine."

She sighed and nodded. *It would have to be,* she thought. She picked up her glass and took a long drink of it, telling herself that Ethan was right and it was all going to work out.

Fifteen minutes later, there was a knock at the door and Ethan opened it to see a chauffeur standing there. He kissed Haley goodbye and headed to the car with the driver.

Ten minutes after that, the doorbell rang and Haley took a deep breath and put a big smile on her face as she opened the door to Enrique Aragon.

He was a tall man, slender but fit, with dark wavy hair to his collar, olive-toned skin, dark eyes, a clean shave, a squared jaw, and a dazzling smile. He walked in the house and took her hand, lifting it to his lips and kissing the back of it softly.

"What a wonderful privilege to finally meet you, Haley." He had a rich Spanish accent. She felt the butterflies in her stomach begin to riot. Her nerves were at it again.

"It's very nice to meet you as well. Would you like a glass of wine, Enrique?" she asked hopefully. He nodded and she walked him to the kitchen, pouring him a big glass and filling up another for herself.

"Where is Mr. Richards?" he asked, looking around and seeing only the camera crew.

Haley's smile fell slightly. "He was called away for an appointment. I'm afraid it's just us," she told him with a bit of disappointment.

He waved his hand subtly. "Not to worry, I am fortunate to spend my afternoon with such a beautiful woman looking at her artistic creations. May I say, Haley, you are absolutely breathtaking in that dress. It's almost as irresistible as you are." He winked at her and held out his arm. "Now then, please indulge me and show me your artwork."

The camera crew followed them through the house as they walked from wall to wall looking at all of it. Enrique complimented her on each piece, discussing it in detail with her, and telling her how much he loved them.

"I am certain that so many of my clients will be anxious to purchase these pieces, and more if you have any that you are working on." He drew near to her and placed his hand low on her back as he stood right beside her. "May I see your studio?" he asked softly, just over her shoulder into her ear.

She got a shiver from the feel of his breath caressing her skin, and she smiled at him and nodded. "Of course, Enrique. I'd love to show you the studio." They walked outside, camera crew in tow, and she opened the door for him, but he insisted that she enter first. She showed him the few pieces that were unfinished and in the works, sitting up on her easels, waiting for her to complete them.

He liked what he saw in there as well, and as they were standing at the last canvas, she realized that as she had been talking about it, he had been staring at her as he stood right beside her.

Haley turned her head to look at him, and felt heat rise up to her cheeks when she met his warm dark eyes. He lifted his hand to touch the curls of her hair, hanging down on the back of her neck in tendrils. He took one between his fingers, and slowly ran his fingertips over the length of it, glancing at it and then looking her in the eyes.

"It is, as I said, so rare to find a woman who possesses such immeasurable beauty, and such profound talent. You arrest my attention, Haley. I thought that you were beautiful when I saw you on television. But seeing you in person... the way the sunlight touches this beautiful mahogany skin of yours," his finger let go of her hair and he touched her cheek softly, tracing his finger slowly down to her chin, "the way the flecks of gold and blue in those mysterious green eyes of yours sparkle, like you are hiding a thousand secrets and delights in them, and this... delicious mouth of yours...." he said quietly as he lifted her chin and touched his lips to hers.

All the wine she had dizzied her and as his mouth touched hers she closed her eyes, reaching for him to steady herself, and he reached his arms around her to steady her, and to pull her close to him. Her mind and body felt like they were on two different roller coasters as she tried to focus on what was happening. He parted her lips with his and she felt his tongue slide over hers as his arms tightened around her. He kissed her deeply, slowly, and sensually, and all the while she was reeling, trying to make sense of it.

Finally, she put her hands on his chest and gave a push, and he kissed her softly once more and then leaned back and looked at her, his hands at her waist as she opened her eyes and blinked at him in astonishment.

"Enrique! I'm married! What are you-" he reached a finger up to her lips and pressed it there gently, silencing her.

"Now, now... we both know it's not a real marriage. We both know that you are only in this for the money. You are already halfway through your time with him, and when it's over, he will go his way, and you will go yours, no? Is that not what you are planning to do? He is not in love with you. He shows it for the camera, but my dear, has he said it? Has he told you that he loves you?" he asked, nearing his face to hers again.

She felt everything in her stop. He was right. It was for the money, and they had planned on going their separate ways when it was all said and done.

"Has he said that he loves you?" he repeated, slipping his arms around her and holding her close to him.

"No..." she whispered, staring into his eyes, almost hypnotized by the wine and heat of the moment between them.

Enrique leaned forward and kissed her softly on the lips again for just a moment, but then leaned back and asked, "Has he said that he wants to be with you after the show is done, or will he go his own way?"

She felt hot tears sting her eyes and she tried to blink them back. Enrique lifted his hand to hold the side of her neck and her jaw as he whispered to her.

"He is leaving you, isn't he... he hasn't said anything about staying together."

She shook her head and closed her eyes for a moment, drawing in a deep breath. "No. He hasn't said anything about staying together."

Enrique leaned toward her and caught her lips in his again, kissing her more sensually as his hand held her head to him for a long minute, and then he looked down at her again.

"What will you do then, my beauty?" he asked, kissing her and moving his lips over her cheek and down her neck to her throat as his hand slid over the side of her breast and down to her hip where it rested low and tight.

"I will be honest with you," he said quietly, looking at her and kissing her mouth once more before continuing. "I want to show your art, and I will put your pieces in my galleries and you will have a future with me professionally, but... I must admit... when your little charade here is done in a few months, I want much more from you than your art. I want your time, and I want you with me."

She gasped and stared at him, trying her hardest to focus on him and stand steady.

"I'm a man of wealth and power, my lovely Haley, and you... you are like a fine and rare work of art. A one of a kind piece that must be treasured and well cared for... loved... indulged... wanted beyond measure," he said passionately as he gazed into her eyes.

"Forgive me if I have been too forward with you today. I could not resist such an enticing woman; such a natural work of art as you," he said. His fingers trailed over the side of her breasts again as he lifted them from her waist and brought them to her neck, pulling her in for another deep kiss, holding her tightly to him.

She reached up and pushed against his chest again, and he let her go and stepped back with a smile. "Give it some thought, will you?" he asked. "I'm a phone call away. I want you, for much more than just your magnificent artwork. I would treasure and cherish you, Haley, and show you passion you have never imagined. I could give you the world, and I want to.

"I will be waiting for you, little dove, but I will not be waiting patiently, especially after tasting your kiss here today. Let me know what you want to do, and we can talk about your art then, too."

Haley took a step backward from him, wanting to avoid another kiss. "I don't know you, Enrique, so I couldn't tell you what I want or don't want later, but I can tell you that I am a married woman right now, and it doesn't matter that it's a reality show marriage, it's still a real marriage. You came here to look at my artwork, and I was glad to share it with you, but don't try to seduce me in my own home while my husband is away.

"That is no way to try to convince me that I should be with you later on. It just shows me that you have no respect for boundaries and marriage. If you want the artwork, you can have it, but you'll have to work a lot harder than that to get me."

She spoke stronger than she felt, but she managed to say what she wanted to stay and to do it without wobbling, though she was still a little dizzy. "You can leave."

He nodded and gave her a little bow. "It was my great pleasure to see you, and I'm looking forward to seeing you again soon," he said simply, and then he turned and walked out of the studio and left the house. The camera crew got every bit of it.

Harvey and Joe looked as if they were ready to take Enrique down. Harvey went to Haley and helped her to the sofa in her studio. "Too much wine, missy. Too much wine. I know you were nervous, but that didn't put you in a good position with him. I was about one more minute from laying him out cold on the floor.

"I have to let you make your own decisions and I'm not supposed to intervene in anything, but he was much too close to crossing a serious line with you, and I want you to know, Joe and I wouldn't have let him do it."

Haley nodded gratefully. "Thanks, Harvey and Joe, I appreciate it."

The camera crew sat with her a while and then helped her back to the house, where she laid down and fell asleep in her room.

Chapter8

Ethan walked through the door of Murphy's office and Murphy looked up at him and smiled slightly. "Our own Norse God. Good. Sit down." He nodded at the chair before his desk.

Ethan sat. "What's the emergency?" he asked Murphy in a worried voice.

Murphy looked him dead in the eyes. "The ratings are slipping too much. We need to stir things up. I want you to meet with Erica at a hotel and I want you to screw her. Cameras on. I want as much footage of you screwing her brains out as we can legally put on television."

Ethan's mouth fell open and he blinked in shock. "I can't do that!" he objected in amazement at Murphy's audacity.

"You can do that. The ratings need a boost. You are under contract," Murphy told him calmly.

"I don't feel like that would be good for the show at all. I don't think it would help your ratings one bit. This is supposed to be a show about Haley and I falling in love, isn't it?" he asked incredulously. He didn't know how he felt about either one of them at that point, and he wasn't about to make a move in either direction. Especially under orders.

Murphy leaned forward and sighed as if he was being patient, explaining things to a man who should have understood them already. "Ethan, she is your girlfriend. You love her. Go screw her brains out; I'm paying you to do it. It doesn't get better than that."

Ethan shook his head. "I can't do that."

Murphy raised his voice slightly. "You can do that, and you will do that, or you will leave the show, you will not get the money, and Haley will not get her money. Don't argue with me, you are working for me."

Ethan stared at him. "You'd end the show over this? You'd take the money? We've done everything you asked us to!" He lowered his brows at Murphy.

"I'm warning you. Do not argue with me. Erica is going to call you. When she calls you, you get in the car she sends for you, you go to the hotel, you rock her wild, little world, you get every dirty bit of it on camera, and then you go back to Haley. Do you understand me? If you don't do it exactly like that, you are gone. Off the show. Immediately fired. No show, no house, no money for you, no money for Haley, not a snowball's chance in hell of ever getting another job in this industry.

"You want to lose Haley's money for her? Go ahead and tell me no. Otherwise, there are only two words I want to hear come out of your mouth before you leave my office. Yes, sir. That's it." He leaned back in his chair and slammed his hands down on the armrests, his eyes locked on Ethan.

Ethan couldn't risk losing Haley's money just because he was torn on what to do. He gritted his teeth and stood up, looking down at the worm of a man sitting at the desk before him.

"Yes, sir," he almost growled, and then he turned and walked out of the door, slamming it behind him.

The whole way home, he was torn between what he felt he ought to do, and what might be right and what might be wrong. Everything had seemed so clear in the beginning. He had a girlfriend, she wanted money to go to New York, he got married and had every intention of divorcing Haley the moment the show ended and the money was in his account.

Then he and Haley grew to be friends and he made love with her, love like he had never experienced, and he felt as though Erica was perhaps fading away for him, but he wasn't sure if it was because they had spent so much time apart or because they had never really been that connected and close.

Now he didn't know what he was going to do when the show ended. He didn't know if he would go back to Erica, or go out on his own, or even if there might be some slight chance that he and Haley might work out somehow and he could be with her.

What he did know was that Murphy was forcing him to screw Erica for ratings. Of course, he wouldn't let a hundred grand go for himself or for Haley; he couldn't cost her that amount of money. He felt frustration growing in him. Erica was his real girlfriend, so there wasn't anything at all wrong with him sleeping with her, was there? Except he was in a fake, and yet real, marriage to Haley, and he didn't want to hurt her.

They had gotten so close; he didn't know if she would be hurt if he slept with Erica. He hadn't even told her that he and Erica were planning on being together after the show was over. He wasn't even sure if that was still the plan, at least for him. Erica was sure it was the plan. What had she told him? Eyes on the money... don't get wrapped up in the girl...

Ethan pulled into a flower shop, bought a dozen red roses in a beautiful crystal vase, and placed them carefully in the car. He felt he owed at least that to Haley. He was committed to cheating on her in their marriage now, if it was a marriage.

He walked into the kitchen and set the roses down on the counter. Harvey and Joe were sitting at the breakfast bar on the island, each of them with a cup of coffee in front of them.

Ethan frowned slightly. It was a rare thing to see the two men of his camera crew sitting down to coffee instead of walking around with the camera and sound equipment.

"Where is Haley?" Ethan asked curiously.

Harvey sipped his java and set the mug down softly. "She's sleeping. She had a little too much wine."

Ethan was surprised. "Is she okay?"

"Yeah, she's alright. She's going to feel like hell when she wakes up, though."

"Did the art dealer show up?" Ethan asked them both.

Joe and Harvey exchanged a loaded glance. "Yeah, he showed up alright," Joe told Ethan. "He likes her art. We'll let you tell her about it."

Ethan sighed. "Alright." He fixed himself a sandwich and then told the guys, "I'm probably just going to head to bed early. If it's allowed, you two could knock off for the night and we will see you in the morning."

Harvey nodded. "Yeah, I don't think she's going to get up before tomorrow morning anyway. We'll see you then."

Joe and Harvey stood up and rinsed out their coffee mugs and placed them in the dishwasher. Haley had them trained just as well as she had Ethan trained. The crew said goodnight and left.

Ethan walked around the house and looked at the walls where they had hung her art. There were several pieces that he really loved, some he didn't feel either way about, and a few that he hoped she never sold, or if she did sell them, that he could be the one who bought them.

He hoped it had gone really well for her, and he supposed that she might have had too much to drink purely out of nerves and then celebration. He walked into their room, pulled his clothes off, put them in the hamper, and then laid down beside her in the bed, cuddling up close to her and holding her as she slept.

As he drifted off to sleep, he wondered at the mess he was in, and tried to figure out what the best possible scenario would be.

Morning light touched them hours later and she awoke nestled in his arms. He was already awake, not having slept much. He had been watching her sleep, considering everything that was tangled so much in his mind.

"Good morning." She came to and realized that her head felt like it might explode. She was also tremendously dehydrated.

"Good morning," he answered her back. "How are you feeling?"

"Like a train wreck," she mumbled.

He chuckled a little. "That's alright, it'll be gone soon. How did it go with the art dealer?"

She didn't want to think about how it had gone. He had come on strong to her and he wanted to date her and sell her art. She didn't feel like telling her husband that he had kissed her several times and made a couple of passes at her. "He likes my art. He wants to sell it," *and take me away from you*, she thought.

"How did your meeting with Murphy go?" she asked him quietly, closing her eyes shut tight against the brightening light.

He frowned. "It was just some more red tape for the show," he mumbled quietly. "Let me ask you this," he said a bit more clearly, "what are you planning on doing with your money when the show is over?"

Ethan reached up and began to rub her shoulders gently, and she smiled to herself a little and relaxed some. "I'm going to open my own gallery and have enough money to be able to paint full time for a couple of years. I'm so excited for it, I can hardly wait. It's a real dream come true for me," she said with a blissful sigh.

It was like a knife in Ethan's heart. He knew he couldn't take that away from her. The only choice left open to him was to screw Erica when she called, whenever that might be. He didn't know just what Murphy was planning on doing with the footage, or why he thought it would be any good for the show, but Murphy wasn't going to back down from his demand, and Ethan felt like he couldn't do anything other than exactly what Murphy wanted him to do.

Especially costing Haley her dream and her future. *If it was only him who would suffer, if it was only him who might lose the money,* he thought, *then maybe,* but then he realized that it was the most selfish thing he could do, backing out of it. If he slept with Erica, she would get his money as she had wanted from the beginning, Haley would get her money, and they would all be alright.

He was the only one with the very strange issue; not certain of wanting to sleep with his own girlfriend. The more he thought about it, the more he realized there was no other choice for him.

"What are you going to do with your money?" she asked him as she turned her head to him and opened one eye to look at him.

He sighed. "Give it someone who needs it more than I do." It was why he had done it all to begin with.

Haley grinned at him. "You are the sweetest, kindest, most thoughtful and generous man I have ever known."

He pulled her close to him and kissed her forehead. He wondered if she would still think that if she ever found out that he was going to screw another woman for the money. He was certain that she would lose all respect for him. As he imagined her hurt heart and her response to the truth of the whole outcome of the show, he knew she ought to take her money and leave. She should begin her life as a gallery owner, make and sell her art, and he would go his own way, after giving his money to Erica as he had told her he would do.

It seemed that hypocrisy ruled his life just then. The best solution for him would be to make himself let go of the feelings he had for Haley, so that when the time came to say goodbye to her, it would be easier to let her go. He could not leave her easily if he was in love with her, and at the rate he was falling for her, it wouldn't take long before he was too in love with her to let her go. He decided he would have to make himself fall out of love with her, somehow, and as quickly as possible.

He began to keep a slight distance from Haley, and at first she didn't notice it right away, but over the few days that followed his meeting with Murphy and her afternoon with Enrique, it became evident to her that he wasn't touching her quite as often. He was absent from her company more than usual, and at night, he would turn away from her and sleep, rather than hold her and make love with her. He kissed her forehead or her cheek, rather than her lips, and when he spoke to her, he didn't often look her in the eye.

She wondered what it could be, and then she realized that perhaps he had found out about how Enrique had come on to her, kissed her, held her, and touched her. She was so miserable that she couldn't make herself talk to him about it, she could only let him keep his distance and it hurt her heart.

Harvey and Joe noticed it as well, and they caught the change on the camera; nothing hides from the lens, Harvey had told them at the beginning, and he was right.

A couple of days later, Ethan was swimming in the pool, his head underwater, as Haley painted in her studio near him, with the door open. She heard his phone begin to ring, and after a few rings, she poked her head out of the studio and saw that he was doing laps. She knew he couldn't hear it, and she didn't want him to miss a call, so she went to the table where his phone was and answered it.

"Hello?" she asked.

There was the soft laugh of a woman on the other end of the line. "This must be the little Mrs.," the woman said.

"This is Haley. May I help you?" she asked, trying to hide her annoyance at the comment by the woman on the other end of the line.

"Well, hello... Haley. Would there happen to be a gorgeous, tall, blonde, hunk of a man who is a rock star in bed, around there somewhere?" the woman asked in a sultry, catty voice.

Haley was sure that she didn't like the woman. "Who is this?" she asked in irritation.

The woman laughed again. "This is the woman he was going to marry before he married you. I'm the love of his life, and he calls me baby, but you can call me Erica."

Haley narrowed her eyes and her voice grew deep and dangerous. "Listen, Erica..." she said with a slightly nasty tone, "I don't know who you are or what you want, but you don't have any business calling here and asking to-"

"Ohhhhhhh.... he hasn't told you. Isn't that sweet. He probably doesn't want to hurt your little heart. Either that or he is still interested in screwing you and wants to keep his options open."

"I don't know what you're talking about-" Haley began, but Erica interrupted her.

"That much is obvious. Is my lover there, or do I leave a message for him to call me back?" she asked dryly.

Haley grew irate. "Okay Erica, that's enough out of-" she was cut off again, this time by Ethan, who was standing next to her, dripping water everywhere. He pulled the phone from her hand quickly and frowned at her.

"What are you doing answering my phone?" he asked in frustration.

Haley felt suddenly that she had intruded much further than she ever should have gone.

"I'm sorry." She turned toward her studio, her heart aching as she walked away from him, wondering why such a wretched woman was calling him and if she really was all the things to him that she said she was. Haley headed back to her studio and closed the door behind her as tears rolled down her cheek.

She closed her eyes and told herself that she had no business holding Ethan to any kind of standard, after all, hadn't she stood right in that same studio as another man kissed her? Haley opened her eyes and wiped the tears off her cheeks. Her marriage was nothing more than a temporary situation; a brief blip in her life, and that was all. A paid job.

She had just let it get too deep, and let it get to her, because she had let her feelings for Ethan overwhelm her, but she either had to tell him that she cared about him, or let him go so that when it was all over, she wouldn't get her heart broken.

She didn't know if he would believe that she cared about him, especially after she strongly suspected that he knew about Enrique's advances to her during his visit, but she felt as though she had to at least give it a chance. She turned around to go out to him and saw that he was gone from the pool. She frowned and looked around. He was nowhere to be seen.

Haley walked into the house looking for him, and found him walking out of the shower, his body dewy and warm, as he stood nude before her, toweling his hair. She drew in her breath. He always took her breath away when he was like that.

"I... I thought we could talk," she tried to say without fumbling too much.

His eyes avoided hers, as they had been doing for days. "I can't. I have to go to a meeting," he said as he dressed in snug jeans and a button down shirt.

She knew that he didn't want to talk to her. "Who are you meeting with?" she asked curiously.

He turned away from her. "Just someone for the show." He sounded angry to her, and she knew from his voice that he did not want to have the conversation with her at all.

"When will you be home?" she asked hesitantly.

He was quiet as he combed his hair. "I don't know. You probably shouldn't wait up for me. Just eat without me, and I'll be back when I'm done."

He walked out of the room and headed to the front door. She walked behind him, watching him go, and feeling somehow like she wouldn't have to wait until the end of the season; she felt like she had already lost him. As she turned sadly away from the door, hugging herself, she caught a glimpse of Harvey and Joe filming her, both of them frowning. Harvey packed up the camera quickly, and Joe followed him out of the door.

Ethan drove to the hotel where Erica had told him to go. He sat outside in the parking lot when he parked, biting his thumb, thinking carefully about what he was doing. He hated it. He hated seeing Haley's face when he left, he hated thinking about how his illicit sexual tryst with Erica was going to hurt her and he knew in his heart that it would.

He hated that he would have to live with it for the rest of his life. He hated that Murphy was making him do it, that he felt like he had no choice, and he hated most of all that if he didn't do it, he was going to cost them both their money and the show.

He felt a little bad for Erica; she didn't know that they were being used and were pawns in a trap. She didn't know that the money was on the line. She didn't know that he had been considering not returning to her after the show was over, or that he had begun to truly fall in love, real love, with Haley.

He sighed and dropped his head into his hands. There was just no way out of it. He shook his head once, and then got out of his vehicle and closed the door, locking his car. He lifted his strong chin and walked into the hotel.

When he got to the suite on the top floor where Erica had told him to go, he was surprised to see such a huge and beautiful room, and he was enormously ashamed to see Harvey and Joe standing there with the camera and sound equipment. They didn't look at him, and he did not look at them.

Erica wrapped her arms around him, holding him to her and kissing him hotly for a long moment before stepping back and grinning at him. She was wearing a sheer black robe that hung to her feet. She wasn't wearing anything else. Her red hair was full and wavy around her head and her shoulders, hanging down her back, and her robe was open to the waist, offering a generous view of her large breasts.

"There's my lover. The little Mrs. let you out of the house, did she? Did you tell her you were going to come find salvation between my legs?" She laughed at him and walked toward him again, taking his face in her hands and kissing him hard.

"Baby, I really missed you. It's so good to see you. I should have been having a hot affair with you this whole time. Just think of all the hot sexy fun we've missed! Well, that's okay, baby, you can come make it up to me right now." She purred as she grinned at him and reached for his shirt, unbuttoning it slowly and licking and sucking on the skin that was revealed with each new open button.

Ethan didn't say anything to her, he just let her stand there and take his shirt off, moving her mouth and her tongue over his chest. For the first time ever, it didn't turn him on as it always had. When his shirt hit the floor, she lifted her mouth to his again and kissed him deeply, turning her tongue over and around his, as she held firmly to him. He didn't put much effort into kissing her back and she pulled her mouth from his and looked at him sharply, though she smiled as she did it.

"You better give some of this back to me, baby. This camera crew isn't here for nothing. If you want to make it believable, you're going to have to give me a lot more passion." She narrowed her eyes at him. "You could at least act like you wanted to be here with me like this."

He sighed and closed his eyes, knowing she was right, and in the next moment he picked her up in his arms and carried her to the enormous bed, laying her on her back on it and moving above her.

She smiled and wrapped her bare legs around him, grinning up at him. "There's my lover boy," she said triumphantly.

He lowered his mouth to hers and kissed her hard and hungrily, twisting his tongue around hers as he slid his fingers up behind her head into her thick red hair, knotting them in it and pulling her head backward as he ran his tongue down her neck, sucking and biting at her.

"Oh! God! Baby... yes!" she cried out, clamping her hands to his shoulders and digging her nails into his skin.

Ethan reached for her robe and pulled it aside, exposing her breast, and then he gasped it tight in his hand and lifted it to his mouth, sucking and biting fiercely at her nipple as he squeezed it. He began to rock his pelvis against hers and she felt his erection on her and grinned, moving her hands to his hips and pulling him against her tighter.

"Take your pants off, baby, I want you inside me!" She cried out desperately, reaching her hand down and tugging at his zipper and the button on his jeans. He felt her hand on his hardened skin and reached down between their bodies to grab her wrist, bringing it back up by her head and pinning her to the bed.

"Not yet," he told her gruffly and she shivered happily beneath him and lifted her hips to rub herself against his jeans.

He went back to kissing her mouth, her neck, and her breasts as he moved himself against her body, making her writhe beneath him in tormented desire. The camera was on them, on every single thing they were doing.

Ethan stopped suddenly as she cried out in need for him, and he looked down into her green eyes.

"Do you love me?" he asked her bluntly. It had occurred to him that they were just having sex, just like they always just had sex, except that for him he had always felt that he was loving her, or in love with her, or both. She had never said it to him, not in all the times they had been together, in all the times he had told her that he loved her, she had never actually said it back to him.

He had to know. He had to know before they went any further, before he took his pants off and entered her, before he even kissed her again, he had to know if she had any love for him at all in her heart, because suddenly, that was going to make all the difference in the world to him.

She stopped wriggling her hips against him and stared up at him in surprise. "What?" she asked him in confusion.

"You heard me, Erica. Do you love me?" he asked again, more certain the second time he said it that this was going to be the turning point for everything and it all weighed on her response.

She gave him a half-hearted smile and shrugged. "What's that got to do with anything? Huh? We're so good for each other, you and me, baby. We are hot together, and we're beautiful. We don't have to worry about love and all the crap that goes with it. We just have you and me, and we have the best sex anyone has ever had, don't we? Isn't that enough? Couldn't that just be enough?" she pouted at him in frustration.

He shook his head and pushed himself up away from her, and off the bed. "No, Erica, that isn't enough. You know, I used to think that it was, but now I can see that all you ever wanted me for was sex and money, and maybe to show off now and then as a little arm candy."

"What the hell is wrong with that?" she asked in irritation, sitting up and looking at him angrily, her breasts exposed and her legs still spread open. He shook his head at her. "You're so far gone you don't even know what the hell is wrong with that! I can't believe I ever loved you! You are the most selfish, egotistical, self-centered bitch I ever knew! I'm out of here. I'm not going to screw you for the money. I'm getting fired from the show, there is no money now, and you can find your own way to New York or ask Uncle Randall to fund it for you. I'm not paying for it, and I'm not going with you. We're done."

She glared at him in hatred. "He's not my uncle, he's a rich old man I've been sleeping with behind your back!"

Ethan's mouth fell open. He truly hadn't figured it out, but the moment she said it, it was obvious to him. "Then that makes you a hooker." He shook his head and turned away from her, walking toward the door.

She rushed after him, reaching for him. "Don't you dare leave me here like this! Don't you dare lose that money! You get your ass back here and finish this deal we made! You owe me that money you son of a bitch!" she shouted at him as he slipped out of her grasp and walked out of the door, slamming it behind him.

The camera crew followed him, and he saw them in the lobby of the hotel as he was exiting the elevator and buttoning the last button on his shirt. They walked out of another elevator and he looked over at them.

Harvey and Joe both nodded at him and Harvey gave him a thumbs up. "Good call, Ethan," he said. "You did the right thing, no matter what. Now go home. Your wife is alone and she needs you."

Chapter 9

Ethan walked into the house feeling horrible, and at the sound of the door closing, Haley came to him, searching his face, though at a distance. He was quiet and he looked away from her in shame.

"How did your meeting go?" she asked quietly, watching him and wishing he would look at her. She was sure that he was avoiding her eyes because he was so disgusted about what happened with her and Enrique.

He shook his head slightly. "It didn't go as well as it was expected to. I really don't want to talk about it," he said in a low voice, walking around her and heading for the bedroom. He closed the door behind him and she stared at it for a long moment, wishing things were different between them.

She knew he needed the space so she left him alone and went out to her studio to paint in silence.

Ethan immersed himself in a steaming shower and no matter how hot the water was or how much soap he used, he could not clean away the dirty feeling he had deep inside him, or the knowledge that he had cost them each their hundred thousand dollars. It made him nauseous.

He didn't care about losing his; it was going to be for Erica anyway at the beginning; he had never intended to keep any of it for himself, but when he learned how she really felt about him, he knew she didn't deserve it at all. He wasn't sorry she wouldn't be getting any money from him.

The real loss and guilt of it all was that Haley wouldn't have her money, and she wouldn't be able to start her own gallery and have the ability to paint and do her artwork for the coming years. She would have to find another low paying job and keep working at that, only painting here and there in her spare time and trying to get galleries to show her work, unless the gallery owner who came by the house showed it, and then she might have a chance at getting her foot in the door.

He couldn't believe that Erica had been lying to him about Uncle Randall. No uncle at all, just a rich, dirty old man she was screwing for his money and gifts. There was pain and anger in his heart; for the love she had never returned, for the lies she told, for the way she treated him, for everything he had done for her that she had soaked up and used him for over all of their time together.

He couldn't believe that he had loved her and that he had wanted to work so hard to please her. Still, if he hadn't been trying to please her, he never would have met Haley, and he wouldn't have ever known what real love felt like, except that now that he had it, he had lost it, and that knowledge and pain was far greater than any Erica had given him.

Erica might be gone and out of his future, but that didn't change the fact that he had cost Haley a hundred thousand dollars and she wasn't likely to want to be with him when she found out that her future was destroyed because of him, because he was selfish and didn't want to sleep with his girlfriend.

It was going to rip his heart out when she found out and walked away from him, never wanting to talk to him again. He couldn't have helped falling in love with her, but he promised himself that he would do his best to fall out of love with her before he was too deep in love to change it.

   ***

Haley's phone rang the next day and she answered the call, knowing it was from Murphy.

"Hello" she said unenthusiastically.

"Good morning, Haley. I want you to come into my office right away. We have a serious matter to discuss immediately." He sounded firm and unwavering as always.

She sighed. He was so demanding. "Okay, I can come over now." She hung up the phone and stepped out of her studio, looking over at the pool where Ethan was doing laps. She walked up to the edge of it and called his name, kneeling down close to the water.

He surfaced and ran his hand over his face, wiping the water away. His eyes didn't quite reach hers. "What's up?" he asked coolly.

"Murphy called. I have to go see him." She wished that he didn't hate her for what had happened. She felt bad enough about Enrique without Ethan keeping such a distance and being so aloof with her.

He was quiet a moment and nodded. "You be careful around him. The man's a monster." Then he dove back into the water. She watched him shoot through the glossy blue ripples and wished with everything in her that she could reach him again as she once had. She knew that what they had shared was changed, and it seemed unrecoverable because of her indiscretion with Enrique.

She stood up and walked away from him, and as she walked into the house, she didn't see his head lift from the water and watch her as she disappeared.

Murphy looked up from his desk when she walked through his doorway. She was not pleased to see him. He indicated the chair in front of his desk.

"Have a seat."

She sat before him. "Why am I here?" she asked, leveling her gaze at him.

He leaned back in his chair and tilted his head a little, eyeing her for a long moment, and then he swung forward and laid his arms on his desk, his eyes steady on hers.

"The ratings for the show are down and we need to yank them back up fast. We have to pull a quick stunt to make that happen, and the duty falls to you to do it." She frowned and curiosity rose in her just a bit. "What is it that you think my duty is?"

Murphy smiled slowly at her, his mouth spreading wide like a frog. "I saw the tape of your little tryst with the art dealer... Enrique whatever his name is. There you were making out with him in your cute little studio. Cheating on your new husband."

Haley's mouth fell open and she drew in her breath in surprise.

"It turns out, the public likes that kind of thing. It makes them feel better about themselves." He shrugged. He didn't care what they thought of themselves, but he was interested in feeding them what they wanted to see.

She pursed her lips together and narrowed her eyes. "What do you want from me, Murphy?" she asked, knowing deep in her heart that she really didn't want to know what he wanted from her.

"I want you to call the guy back up. I want you to tell him you'll date him. I want you to go out with him and have dinner, go dancing, spend a hot afternoon between his sheets with nothing between you but sweat. I want it all on camera. I want a hot, lurid, sexy affair between you and him, and I want it immediately." He didn't even blink.

Haley stared at him. "How can you possibly ask me to do that? You just told me last time I was here that you want me sleeping with Ethan and going over the top romantic with him for the cameras!"

Murphy rolled his eyes, "Don't be dramatic, it's obvious that doing that wasn't a problem for you. You're married to him, everyone wanted it, now everyone is bored and they want hot, tawdry, illicit sex outside of your house and outside of your marriage."

She shook her head. "He's not a decent man. He came on to me while I was intoxicated and he knew I was married. He didn't care. I'm not doing anything with him."

Murphy frowned and leaned toward her. "I don't care what he did or why, what I care about is ratings. You are going to pick up your phone and call him, you are going to tell him that you haven't been able to stop thinking about him since he left, you're going to tell him that your little make out session with him left you hot for him and you're going to beg him to see you.

"Tell him you want him, and tell him you can't wait until the season is over. Beg him to take you now, and to keep it a secret. Appeal to his ego. Tell him how gorgeous and wealthy and sexy he his, and how his kiss left you panting for more. Tell him you're dreaming about him and you need him and you can't go another day without him."

Anger bubbled hotly inside of her as she fully grasped what he wanted her to do.

"Date the man, screw him wherever and whenever you can, every chance you can, and get all of it on film! Now!" he demanded, his eyes locked on her.

She shook her head and rose to the edge of her seat. "I'm not going to do it, Murphy! You can't make me do it!"

He shrugged. "You're right. I can't make you do it. What I can do is fire you from the reality show and deny you the hundred thousand dollar prize money at the end, and then I can fire Ethan and deny him the hundred thousand that he had coming to him." He leaned even closer and leered at her.

"Do you want to explain to Ethan that you were fooling around with another man, making out with him and leading him on like a little tease and then you backed off and decided to just throw away everything you have both worked for all of these months, including costing him his job, his reputation and his hundred thousand dollars? He won't be able to work in this town again." Murphy slammed his hand down on his desk to punctuate his point.

She felt a wave of nausea rise up in her and threaten to make her vomit right on his desk. She couldn't cost Ethan his job or his share of the money. She didn't care about her part of it; she'd rather let it go than sleep with a man like Enrique, but she wasn't about to cost Ethan his share if she could help it. She just didn't think she could do it. She didn't think she could make herself sleep with him.

"I can't do it! It's going to ruin our show!" she said bitterly, trying to hold in the tears that had begun to sting her eyes. "I've done everything else you have asked me to do, right from the very beginning, but I can't do this!" she shook her head adamantly.

His lip curled back and he spoke in a cold and cruel voice. "You'll do it, and you'll do it fast, or you will lose both your job and Ethan's, and you will lose both of your reward money for finishing the show. I'm giving you until the next show to spread your legs for that man, or you're both done. Do you understand me? I want all of it, on camera. Now."

Less than one week. That was no time at all, she thought as she stared in horror at the man before her. Ethan was right. He was a monster.

She bit her lip, holding in all the confusion and frustration she felt, wishing with all of her heart that she could just vanish from the spot she was in. He looked up at her expectantly.

"Go do it. Or leave and end the show now." He leaned back in his chair as if that was the final word and she stared at him and shook her head silently, not knowing what to say or do. She wanted to tell him off. She wanted to tell him what a rotten demon he was and how she hoped he rotted in hell, but she did not have the luxury of freedom to say something like that to him without it costing Ethan.

She turned on her heel and stormed out of the office, slamming the door behind her. All the way to her car, she held her fury and frustration in, but the moment the door closed, she dissolved into tears, weeping over what she could not control and had no real choice in deciding.

She couldn't sleep with Enrique, she couldn't even begin to stomach the idea, but she couldn't cost Ethan the money he was working so hard for by doing the show. She was stuck between a rock and a hard place and it was going to cost her either her morals or what was left of the shreds of her bond with him and his money.

She cried until she was cried out, trying to think of a way, any way that she could get out of both scenarios, but nothing came to her. She finally got her breath back, cleaned up her lovely face, and drove home. When she walked into the kitchen, she found Ethan cooking a soup and baking fresh bread.

He didn't look up from the soup, but he spoke to her with a curious voice.

"How was the meeting with Murphy?" he asked almost as if he didn't want to really know.

"It was just some details he wants to me to change and work on." She sighed. "I really don't want to talk about it." She could not even stand to think about it, let alone discuss it.

They were quiet, and the conversation was strained between them. Harvey and Joe both looked on with faces wreathed in disappointment. Each of them had a bowl of soup, a salad, and some bread for dinner.

"Are you working on anything new in the studio?" Ethan asked offhandedly.

She shrugged. "I am poking around with a few things, but nothing specific. Nothing I'm going to finish anytime soon," she answered quietly.

There was no further conversation. The meal ended, the dishes were put away, and even Harvey and Joe knew that there was no reason to keep filming beyond that. They left, and Ethan and Haley went to bed in silence, both of them worried sick over the hell that Murphy put them through. Neither one them could conceive of any viable way out of the messes they found themselves in.

Sleep did not come to them for a long while in their silent room, and no bond could breach the canyon between them in their bed.

Two days later Haley was in her studio staring at a blank canvas, trying to will her muse into inspiring her with some kind of magic for the whiteness staring back at her, when her phone rang and she saw that it was Leslie.

Leslie was well aware of the no-contact rule, and she wouldn't be calling unless it was a dire emergency. As Haley picked her phone up and thought about it, she realized that it didn't matter if she answered her phone or not; that was the least of her worries and she desperately needed the support and help of her friend. She glanced around her and saw that neither Harvey nor Joe was outside with her. She thought they must be inside trying to get some kind of footage with Ethan.

"Hello?" she asked, anxious to hear her friend's caring voice.

"Oh my God, girl... you are not going to believe what is going on. I know I'm not supposed to call you unless it's an emergency, but it is absolutely a full blown red light emergency." Leslie gushed into the phone.

Haley closed her eyes. "It's so good to hear your voice!" she said tightly, trying her best to hold her emotions in while simultaneously letting them out to a trusted friend.

There was a quick moment of silence on the other end of the line and then Leslie realized that something was very wrong. Concern flooded through the phone for Haley and Leslie went right into a stream of questions.

"What's wrong? What happened? Did you already find out?" she asked, firing her barrage.

Haley let the tears fall. "The producer of the show is trying to force me to have sex with a horrible man, and if I don't then he's going to kick both Ethan and I off of the show and neither one of us will get the money. All of this time and work and sacrifice will have been a waste, and I can't sleep with the jerk he wants me to have an affair with, and I can't cost Ethan a hundred thousand dollars! I don't know what to do!" she moaned bitterly.

"What? He can't make you sleep with anyone! What kind of a low life jerk is he?" she demanded angrily. "Don't you do it. You don't have to do a damn thing. Besides, that son of a bitch Ethan doesn't deserve your mercy or worry. Don't you even think for one second about whether or not he ought to get his money. He is such a snake!" she insisted adamantly.

Haley blinked in surprise and wiped the tears from her cheeks. "What are you talking about? What do you mean he's a snake? He's amazing, Leslie, I'm in love with him. I just couldn't help it. He's the most amazing man I've ever met."

Leslie scoffed. "You only believe that because you don't know what happened. Ugh! When I think of you being with him it makes me so mad!"

"Leslie, what are you talking about?" Haley asked in confusion.

"Of course you don't know, you've been locked away in that house with no connection to anyone and no access to the show. That son of a bitch. I know that producer is pulling everyone's string's like they're puppets. It's horrible. Honey, I hope you're sitting down, and I hope you don't really mean it when you say that you are in love with Ethan, because he is nothing but a low down dirty dog. Girl, he's cheating on you, and it is all over the show.

"It's on the commercials, it's one of the hot story lines right now. How you two fell in love, or at least, everyone thought you did, and everyone was so happy for you two, but then the jerks that run this show started showing commercials of Ethan with another woman and then last night on the show, there he was with that other woman, hotter than hot, getting it on with her. I was so mad! How are you doing? Are you alright?" Leslie asked in worry after she calmed down from her rant.

Haley shook her head, completely confused. "Leslie, what are you talking about? Ethan's not having an affair with another woman. He's almost always here at the house with me. It's ridiculous, it's almost like lockdown."

Leslie scoffed. "Oh honey, they have you so fooled. He is having a hot affair with some nasty woman named... oh what was her name... little red headed whore... so full of herself. What was her name?" Leslie asked herself, trying to think of it.

A sick feeling came over Haley. She knew, before it was spoken, exactly who it was, and she suddenly felt like the fool the rest of the nation knew her to be.

"Erica?" she asked dryly as her heart clenched and her face grew hot.

"Yeah! That's it! Wait... how did you know? I thought you didn't know he was having an affair," Leslie asked, getting confused herself.

Haley closed her eyes and rubbed her hand over her forehead. "She called him here at the house and she told me she is the woman that he was going to marry before he married me. She said he was her lover. I thought she was just being catty. I didn't think she was serious. Ethan said it wasn't anything."

She shook her head slowly, realizing just how much a fool she had been, not only to the rest of the nation, but to Ethan and to the producers... to everyone, including Erica. No wonder the woman sounded so sure of herself and so cocky about him.... calling her the little Mrs. Haley. Haley loathed the thought of her.

"Oh honey, he was lying through his teeth to you. I can't believe he said it wasn't anything. You should have seen them! My god! I didn't think they'd show something like that on the television on regular channels; you usually have to pay extra to get channels that show stuff like that. There he was, walking through this office door and she was waiting for him there on the couch, her in her itty-bitty little black skirt.

"They started kissing and it got hot and they went to the couch in the office and she climbed on his lap and ripped her shirt off; she didn't have anything on under it but a black bra, and they were making out so hot and heavy! He was kissing her boobs and rubbing her legs. I'm sure he must have slept with her right after that." Leslie said in disgust.

Haley didn't think she could stand to listen to any more of it. "I don't know when he would have done that." she said quietly. "Maybe one of the meetings he had to go to when I stayed home? I don't know. I can't believe it.

"We haven't been getting along at all, it's been so awful and so quiet here at the house. We aren't talking to each other or looking at each other and I thought it was because he knew about what happened with Enrique, and that he was mad at me. I never thought for a minute that it was because he was having an affair and didn't want me anymore." She hated the taste of the words in her mouth as she spoke them. The realization made her head ache.

"What do you mean what happened with Enrique? Who is he? Have you been having an affair too?" Leslie asked quizzically.

Haley sighed. "So they haven't showed that yet." She couldn't begin to understand what they were doing. "Well, I got a call from an art dealer named Enrique, and he wanted to come over to the house and see my art and talk about putting it in his galleries in Los Angeles and New York. I was so nervous before he came that I had some wine... a lot of wine... and I drank when he got here, and by the time our visit was just about done, I was way past buzzed.

"He made some moves on me, kissing me and trying to get fresh with me, touching me...." The memories made her want to vomit. "He's such a jerk. I pushed him away and told him off, and he left, but he still wants to show my work, and I don't know if I will have him do it or not. I might have to if I get kicked off of this show.

"Anyway, I thought Ethan knew about that and was blaming me for it. I thought he was mad at me for Enrique kissing me, and it turns out he just didn't want me anymore and was busy having a hot fling on the side. Son of a bitch!" she swore. "You know, he wasn't here when Enrique came over. I bet that's when he was off with Erica. Jerk!" she scowled angrily and Leslie chimed in.

"He is a jerk, honey, and he doesn't deserve your love. I wish I could show you the video of him with that woman on the couch, my God, it was the raciest thing. I think the editors cut it off right before they had sex just because they aren't supposed to show stuff like that, but I'll tell you what, that man doesn't care about you at all. Not from what I've seen, and if you saw it, you would know it, too. I wish there was a way to show it to you," Leslie grumbled.

"I don't want to see it. Everyone but me knows. Everything that's been going on here makes perfect sense now. It's all just one big game and I haven't been anything but a pawn and a player in it. That's all. Just one tiny little expendable piece in a big game that isn't about anything but the money and the ratings.

"To think that I was so worried about making sure that he got the money at the end of the show. I was considering sleeping with Enrique because the producers said they weren't going to give either of us the money if I didn't do it!

"They were trying to force me, and I don't care about the money that much, not enough to sleep with Enrique for it, but I was so worried about Ethan not getting his money, not being able to work in Los Angeles again and losing the show, and now I find out all of this. I am so sick. I just can't believe it," she said, just as disgusted as Leslie sounded.

Leslie was quiet for a moment, and then spoke softly. "What are you going to do?" she asked hesitantly.

Haley pursed her lips and shook her head. "I'm going to break up this whole thing. I'm going to tell Ethan off, I'm going to quit the show, and I'm going to get my life back. Every one of them can go to hell. I am done being used and lied to. This is bull. I'm finished here." She let the words move through her; her body, her soul, her heart, her mind, and she knew that she meant them.

"I can't believe I fell in love with a man like that. He's going to take some time getting over, but I am going to start that right now.

Thank you for calling me and telling me, Leslie. You're a good friend. I owe you for this. No one else has said a single word to me." She was grateful for her precious and true friendship, and that was something she could easily see was one of the things in her life that had a real and true value. "I'll call you soon and let you know what's going on, but for now, I am done here."

"Okay! You better call me! Let me know what's going on!" Leslie pleaded.

"I will. Love you, lady," she said and she hung up.

Anger rushed through her and saturated every part of her, making her heart pound and giving her just the strength and energy she needed to face Ethan and Murphy as well. She left her studio, closing the door and looking at it with a broken heart. She had been so charmed by what he had done for her, but it was all a lie. It was a joke, and she was done it; with all of it.

She walked into the house and slammed the door. "Ethan!" she called out.

"In the kitchen."

She went into the kitchen and saw Ethan hovering over the stove, and Harvey and Joe filming him as he was cooking. Harvey looked up at her and smiled until he saw the look on her face, and his face instantly disappeared behind the camera lens.

Ethan looked at her, right in her eyes and saw a fury that he had not seen in her before. He drew a deep breath and froze in place as he took in the situation. She walked toward him and launched all of her anger and pain at him.

"You thought you were going to keep your hot little fling a secret from me? Is that what you thought? All you've done is show the entire nation what a complete and total jerk you are! Well guess what, your sneaking around behind my back just came back and bit you hard. I know all about your little tryst with Erica. Oh yeah, I heard all about it. All the hot little details." She stood just opposite him at the island in the kitchen, glaring at him as her hands splayed on the counter.

Ethan, Harvey, and Joe just stared at her. Ethan blinked and said in a voice just above a whisper, "You know about Erica?"

Haley narrowed her eyes. "Yeah. I know about Erica. Here I was, playing the dutiful little wife to you, believing everything you told me, spending every night in bed with you, falling in love with you, and giving myself to you, and really meaning everything genuinely. All along you were running around behind my back screwing your girlfriend and the whole damn country knew about it, Murphy knew about it, you two knew about it." She flipped her hands at Harvey and Joe who had the grace to look completely ashamed.

"The only person in America who had no idea was poor little old me. I just played the simple little fool for you for months while you were out lying and cheating. You made love with me and you made me believe it! You made me believe that you really were falling in love with me, but it was nothing at all! How dare you do that to me! After everything we have been through and all that I've done for you and given you, and you turn around and do that to me!"

She leaned over further on the counter and Ethan was about to say something to her but she cut him off and he didn't dare interrupt her and make her angrier. Harvey and Joe stood silent and shamed, but they were still recording it.

"You've been acting so cold since the day that Enrique came over here, and this whole time I thought it was my fault. I thought that you were brushing me off and ignoring me because you were angry with me for what happened with Enrique, and I felt so bad about it! I felt so guilty about him coming on to me like he did, and I thought you were hurt and angry and avoiding me because of that, and all this time you were just miserable because you wanted to be with your girlfriend instead of me!

"Then, I went over to talk to Murphy and what does he tell me? He wants me to screw Enrique because the stupid ratings are falling for the show and he thinks if I am cheating on you that it will spike the ratings and everyone will want to watch it. You know what he told me? He said if I don't sleep with Enrique that he's going to fire us both from the show and neither one of us will get any money, and neither one of us will be able to work in this town again.

"I have been agonizing over the decision about dating and screwing Enrique just so you could keep this stupid show and get your money at the end of it, or leaving the whole show, but I just couldn't let you down. Oh no.

"I was putting you first, thinking of you and loving you and I was about to do what Murphy told me I had to do and date Enrique and sleep with him, just so you could keep your job on this show and so you could get your money at the end.

"Then I find out that you're already having an affair on the show. Well guess what, Romeo, I don't care about the show now. I hope it crashes and burns, and I hope your career crashes and burns. There is no way in hell I am staying here in this home, in this marriage, or on this show, and I don't care that we are both going to lose all of that money.

"I couldn't care less! I'm not going to let you use me and make a fool out of me anymore or ever again! I am done! You're going to get divorce papers and you can start looking for another job, because this whole thing is over, right now!"

Ethan wasn't sure if she had even bothered to take a breath, but he had learned so much, just from listening to her, and the first thing he did was drop the spoon in his hand, splattering sauce all over the counter as he ran around the island and rushed to her, grasping her arms and stopping her from leaving.

Harvey and Joe recorded quietly.

"Listen, wait a minute, please. I listened to everything you said, and I didn't interrupt you. I let you say all of it. Now, you need to listen to me because there are things that you don't know and that you have to know before you take another step or say another word. Please!" He looked at her imploringly and she sighed loudly and crossed her arms over her chest.

"What?" she asked smartly, sure that there was nothing he was going to say to her that was going to stop her from walking straight into their room when he was finished, and packing up everything she had and leaving.

He sighed heavily and took a deep breath.

"First of all, you only know part of what is going on. I'm going to be totally honest with you, so I want you to know that right away." He looked at her with wide eyes and she did nothing but watch him silently.

Ethan began. "I was with Erica before I started this show, and it was her idea that I do it. She wanted the money from it so she could move to New York. She talked me into doing it, so yes, when you and I got married, I had no intention of staying married to you, I was going to leave you after the show and take the money and go with her to New York.

"I did talk to her on the phone a couple of times when we were first living together. I wasn't seeing her, though. She and I had talked about it before the wedding, and I wanted to see her on the side, but she wouldn't do it because she wanted me to do this without screwing it up and losing the money, and she wasn't willing to risk losing the money just so she and I could have a sneaky affair.

"I'll be honest with you, at first I was pretty miserable about that. But then, the more I got to know you, the more I cared for you and the more I wanted to be with you, and then things changed between us, and for the first time in my life, I felt love.

"I knew that she didn't love me, that she had never loved me, and I was amazed that I had never realized that she was just using me."

His hazel eyes held hers locked, just as his hands did, and she watched him, her anger still bubbling dangerously.

"Well, you and I went to see Murphy at the office together and he talked to me alone; do you remember that? When he talked to me, he told me that Erica was downstairs right there at the offices and that he wanted me to go have a hot visit with her, just to boost ratings, just one time. I said I didn't want to do it, but he forced me, like he forced you, and I went downstairs and Harvey and Joe were there," he turned around and looked over his shoulder at them, "weren't you, guys?" he asked them for confirmation.

They both looked like the last thing they wanted was to be part of his defense team, but they both nodded subtly and kept filming. Ethan looked back at Haley.

"So I went into the room, not really knowing what to expect and I found Erica there and she kissed me, and I admit, I kissed her back, a lot, and things got kind of hot between us, but there was no sex. I stopped it before that happened.

"I felt bad about it and I didn't want to go further with her. I was pretty sure that whatever it was that Murphy was looking for was taken care of for the show and everything could go back to normal for you and me, because things were just beginning to change for us and it was really becoming important for me to be with you.

"I was falling for you, too. Then not too long after that, after things had really gotten good for you and me and I had decided that I wanted to be with you and not Erica, Murphy called me back in. He called me in on the same day that the art dealer, Enrique, came over here. I went to Murphy's office and he told me that he wanted me to sleep with Erica or he was going to fire us both and not give either one of us the money.

"At that point, I wasn't interested in the money anymore, but I knew how important it was for you to have your part of the money so you could start your gallery, and I didn't want you to lose that opportunity. I couldn't cost you that, so I finally agreed to do what he wanted, and I didn't even know that anything at all happened between you and this Enrique guy until just now when you told me. I'm going to ask you more about that later, but I want to make sure that you know the truth about all of the rest of it, first."

He took a deep breath and Haley began to see the schemes that Murphy had played with them, using them as pawns in a power game against one another. It would guarantee failure and the show wouldn't have to pay out any money at all, but they'd still get a full season with tons of viewers. It was smart, but it was horrible, and it was only centered on the money aspect.

"So when I came back from seeing Murphy, I was so ashamed that I had agreed to sleep with her that I couldn't stand to look at you or touch you. You are so important to me, and I felt like I was letting myself down, letting you down, letting us down, and being turned into a tool by Murphy just to be used for his show. I didn't want to sleep with Erica, but there was no way out of it.

"I was desperate for you to be able to keep your part of the money and be able to open up your gallery when it was over, and Murphy knew it! He played us so well against each other, waiting until he knew that we had fallen in love with each other, and then he told me to sleep with Erica or he would take it all away from us. I was willing to betray my own morality and values so that you could keep your money and build your future.

"I went to meet with her and when I got to the hotel where it was supposed to happen, Harvey and Joe were there," he looked over his shoulder at them again and they nodded sadly, "and I'll be honest, I did kiss her, and things did start to happen with us, but I never even took off my pants. I knew she was just using me and I asked her if she loved me and she didn't; she never has.

"She just wanted to make sure that we got the money, so she was willing to screw me there so we could get to the end of the show and get the money, but when I knew without question that she didn't love me, I left. I fought with her and I told her off and I left and Joe and Harvey here left with me."

Harvey and Joe finally chipped into the conversation then. "That's right!" they added. "We left the same time he did! He never slept with Erica, not the whole time he's been married to you." Harvey told her.

Haley stared at him in surprise and frowned at everything that was finally, slowly coming to light.

"I knew when I left, that Murphy was going to fire us both and that I had cost you your money and mine, and that it was all going to go to hell. I just didn't have the heart to tell you because I wanted to be around you as long as I could before the hammer dropped and we were both let go.

"I just knew you were never going to talk to me again and I wanted to push that day back as far as I could. Then Murphy didn't fire us right away, and I didn't know what was happening, so I was just waiting, but that's when he called you in and wanted you to be with that Enrique art dealer. I don't know what his game is, but he is playing us against each other, and I am not okay with that."

She could see that he was angry, but more than that she could see that he meant every word he was speaking to her.

"I want you to understand some things right now. One, I never slept with Erica. We kissed some, and there was some making out, but it was because Murphy made me do it, and both times I walked out because I didn't want to do it.

"Two, I am not leaving you for her when this is over. No matter what happens when this is over, Erica and I are through. She is a piece of work that I never want to see again as long as I live. Three, my sweet, beautiful, wonderful wife, I love you. I fell in love with you and I couldn't help it. When things got bad between us, I tried to make myself fall out of love with you, but there's just no way it's going to happen. I love you more than any woman I have ever had any kind of feelings for, and I want you for as long as you will let me have you.

"I don't want to get divorced when this stupid show ends; I want to stay married to you for the whole season, and every season of every year for all of our lives until we die. I'm talking old and gray, lady. I want you always. I don't care about the money. It's gone whenever Murphy fires us, and that's that.

"I don't regret any of it, except that you got hurt. I never wanted you to get hurt. Also, I'm pissed at Enrique for coming on to you. I want to hear about that; you are my wife after all, and in my heart, you are really and truly my wife, and no man on this planet should even be looking at you like that, let alone trying to make a move for you."

Haley stared at him and tears formed in her eyes and rolled past her eyelashes and down her cheek. Harvey and Joe were both wiping tears away as well.

Joe spoke up, talking in a soft voice. "Everything he said is true, Haley, every word of it. We can vouch for him, and Ethan, she didn't do anything to make that art dealer want her, he just went after her and she was pretty tipsy that day, so he got a couple of kisses in.

"She didn't even kiss him back, and Harvey and I were about to take him down if he got any closer to her. Then she told him off and kicked him out and we didn't have to step in. She was true to you, Ethan." He nodded at Ethan in confirmation.

Ethan's gaze had shifted to Joe to look at him as he spoke, but when he finished, Ethan looked back at Haley. He took a deep breath and let her arms go, leaning back from her and looking at her.

"Well, I guess the next move is up to you, Haley. I love you, I want you, I didn't cheat on you, and we have no money after we lose this show. That's about all I had to say to you, I guess," he said quietly, waiting for her verdict like a man waiting to be sentenced for life.

She sniffed and shook her head at him. "You are something else, do you know that?"

Then she walked toward him and slipped her arms around his neck and looked up at him. "I love you, too, and I want you for the rest of our lives, too." she told him with a smile, and then she leaned up and kissed him. Joe and Harvey both applauded and wiped tears off their cheeks, and the camera rolled on getting every bit of it.

They sat down at the breakfast bar and talked everything over in more detail, and as the conversation moved through all of the shady tricks that Murphy and the studio had tried to force on them, Harvey and Joe both shared dark and knowing looks with each other, both of them deeply angry over what had happened.

When they had talked through all of it, Ethan looked at Haley and sighed, holding her hand. "Well, Mrs. Richards, what do you want to do about this?"

She didn't even have to think about it. "I want to go into the studio tomorrow morning and quit the show. I want to tell Murphy off and walk out a free woman, at least, with you."

He looked around their beautiful kitchen. "We won't get to keep the house. We lose that right along with everything else. The only things we take with us are the things that we brought when we moved in."

"That's fine with me." she smiled at him. He leaned over and kissed her, and Harvey and Joe looked at each other and nodded.

"We're going to come with you to the studios. That's a conversation that we want to film," Harvey said quietly. "We're going to make it discreet, though. We aren't leaving our jobs, but we can give you some support."

Ethan and Haley agreed, and they planned late into the night.

The Final Chapter

The next morning the four of them went to the studio in two different vehicles and Harvey and Joe went in first, setting up their gear and sending a text to Haley to let her know that they were ready. They were positioned near Murphy's door, close enough that they would be able to record whatever happened in the office without being seen or stopped.

Joe turned on the sound and Harvey turned on the camera, and they got a big surprise. Ethan and Haley came down the hall a moment later and the camera crew hushed them and waved to them to wait outside against the wall and listen.

The camera crew recorded a meeting that none of them were supposed to be privy to.

Murphy was arguing with a fiery redheaded woman in his office and Ethan's mouth fell open when he saw her through the open door and heard her talking. It was Erica.

"I don't care if he didn't have sex with me; you got your video and I did my part in your plan. I broke up their marriage! You said you were going to pay me fifty thousand dollars to do it, and I did it, and you practically have a porn flick now, so I better damn well get paid! You owe me that money, Murphy, and you are going to pay me!" she demanded.

Ethan shook his head. It was what she was good at; demanding things and then getting them.

"You didn't screw him! You were supposed to get him to screw you! I hired Enrique the art dealer to screw Haley, and I hired you to screw Ethan, and neither one of you has made it happen yet!" Murphy raised his voice back at her slightly.

She leaned over his desk, drawing her face and nearly bare breasts up to his face. "Listen, Murphy baby, I just need another chance. I can get Ethan into my bed anytime I want him. He loves it when I screw him. He's addicted to me. He can't get enough of me, and no one knows that better than you." She reached over and took his tie in her hands and slid her fingers over it slowly, toying with it and pulling on it, leading him within a breath of her mouth.

"So, I will get Ethan in bed, I'll screw him and you will give me my fifty thousand dollars. If it doesn't happen like that, you and I can put our heads together and come up with some other way to make sure we both get just exactly what we want. Wouldn't you like that, Murphy?" She tugged harder on his tie, her lips close to his. "To get exactly what you want?"

Murphy's eyes moved from her eyes to her lips and then down to her big breasts, almost falling out of her tight little top. His eyes lingered there and then moved back up to her mouth and then her eyes.

"I'd like that. Just see about screwing Ethan first before you come in here and take me for a ride." He reached his hand to her breast and just before he touched it, she snapped her own hand up to his and stopped him, so close to her bare skin.

She grinned at him. "You have to pay me first, baby," she told him, but then she yanked his tie and pulled him the last inch toward her, and kissed him hard, sliding her hand around the back of his neck and holding him to her mouth, sucking on his tongue and biting him. When she let him go, he looked dazed, and his lips were red with her lipstick.

"You better find a way to get that money for me, and I will go find Ethan and make him come screw me. Video and all. You'll have your little porn for television show, and all your viewers are going to want me instead of that pain in the ass Haley you have on there now."

She stood up and grinned at him, then turned around and walked out. As she passed Ethan and Haley in the hall, Ethan grabbed her arm and she stopped and looked up at him in surprise.

"Ethan!" she gasped, and then she looked at Haley and smirked. "...and the little Mrs. What are you doing here, baby. I was just talking about you with Murphy." She ran her hand up over his chest to his shoulder and smiled at him seductively. "You and I need to get together sometime real soon. Call me, baby." She smiled at him and he yanked her hand from him and flung it aside.

"Don't touch me, whore. I don't ever want to see you or talk to you again. This is it for you and me, right here, right now. I can't believe I was with you for as long as I was. I can't believe that I gave you all that I did, but you know what? Thanks to your greed, making me come on this show, I met and married the woman that I want to spend the rest of my life with, and she and I are very much in love and glad to be with each other.

"So I suppose I ought to thank you, just once, for inadvertently introducing me to the love of my life. You haven't actually met this wonderful woman, have you? Erica, this is my wife, Haley. Haley, this is the woman who enabled us to be together, happily married for the rest of our lives. Erica, I never want to hear from you again. Ever."

With that, he turned his back on Erica, who was beginning to scream at them that their marriage was a joke, and Ethan and Haley walked into Murphy's office unannounced and left the door open for Joe so he could get all of the sound.

Murphy looked up at them from his desk and his eyebrows raised slightly. "Well, I didn't expect to see you two in here today. What's going on?"

They sat down in front of him and Ethan glared at him and started his tirade.

"We're leaving the show effective immediately. You can take your backstabbing, cheating, lying plans, and go to hell." He spoke seriously with a hint of underlying anger.

Murphy looked at them in shock. "No! No... don't do that. We have a lot going on with the show right now, we still have the rest of the season to finish. You have contracts with us, you know, and you can't just walk out on those."

Ethan grew more angry with him. "You changed our contracts by bringing Erica and Enrique into the situation! You tried to manipulate us! You played us against each other and tried to get us to cheat on each other! You said this show was about people figuring out if they could fall in love in what amounted to an arranged marriage, not getting them married to each other and then manipulating their lives so much that both of them go down in flames that wreck their lives!

"You tried to force us through guilt and obligation to have sex with people we didn't want to have sex with! That's illegal and immoral as hell! You lied to us about what you were doing on the show, about what you were doing with each of us, and about what you were going to do with our situations, contracts, and futures!" Ethan's voice was strong and firm.

Murphy closed his eyes for a moment and held his hands up. "Okay. Okay, okay, okay... you got me on some of this. The art dealer isn't really an art dealer, he is an actor that we brought in to play a role in the show. That's all. He was acting! Erica... she too is an actor that we brought in for the same reason. It was..." he paused as he looked from one of them to the other, "You know what it was? It was a test. We wanted to show the viewers that your love was true, and you both passed the test! The viewers love it, and they love you! You can't leave."

"You tried to force us to sleep with other people, Murphy!" Haley almost yelled at him in anger, and Ethan held her hand in his and stroked his fingers over her skin in a calming manner.

"Yeah, well... I'm just following orders, you know. It has to do with ratings. It's all about the ratings. That's all it is. I just take orders from the Executive Producer and he tells me what needs to happen, and I make it happen. That's how it works. So we were just doing what we were told to do by the higher ups. That's all. I'm in this with you both. We are a team.

"You kids can ride out the end of the season... so easy, it'll be a breeze. We'll show you two back together again and you still have your chance at the money at the end of the year. Right? Just ride the season out." He nodded at them, smiling like a car salesman at the end of a short month.

Ethan looked at Haley and she pursed her lips and shook her head. "That's not going to work for us," she said with a deep and quiet anger, her eyes nearly burning with fury at Murphy.

Murphy looked away from her and he met Ethan's gaze. "Think of the money. Each of you would get one hundred thousand dollars!"

Ethan shook his head. "We don't want it, Murphy. It's not worth putting up with all of your lies and backstabbing and trickery to try to get that money at the end... to have a chance at it. Too much. We are done. We are quitting as of right now, and you can figure out your own show and do with it whatever you like, but we are finished, and this is it. Let the contracts go or we are going to get attorneys and sue you for everything we can possibly come up with."

Murphy frowned angrily at him. "You want to leave? You want to blow your chance at ever working in television again? You are going to lose the money, and you're going to lose the house. You're going to ruin your reputations. You're going to be the laughing stock of the whole nation! Is that what you want?" he raised his voice, scowling at them both.

They stood up to leave. "We don't want any of that. We got true love, and that's what your show was supposed to be about to begin with."

The two of them turned and walked to the door, and as they reached it they both looked back at the miserable man sitting behind the desk. "Goodbye,

Murphy." Then they walked down the hall and he banged his fist on the desk in front of him.

Ethan and Haley turned to look behind them at the end of the hall and they saw Harvey and Joe walking down the hall toward them. Harvey winked at them and Joe gave them the thumbs up sign.

They left the studio and Haley and Ethan went back to the house and packed up their belongings. He helped her take down all of her artwork. There was quite a bit more of it than there had been when she had first moved in. She had been hard at work since Ethan had built her studio for her.

She was sad to see her studio emptied and she stood outside of the door, looking in at it with a pout when it was empty. She felt Ethan come up behind her and slide his arms around her waist, holding her back against his chest. He leaned his chin down to her shoulder, kissing it softly.

"I'll build you another one someday soon." he whispered in her ear. "That's a promise. A bigger, better, more perfect studio."

She smiled a little, but the pout still held its place at the corner of her mouth. She turned in his arms and hugged him back. "I know, but this was the first one you made for me. It's one of the reasons I fell in love with you."

"Well then, let's leave it with a happy memory." He smiled at her, taking her hand and leading her to the sofa that was set against the back wall. He lowered himself down onto the sofa and pulled her down with him, kissing her softly and before long, the kissing led to sweet love, and they made a wonderful parting memory in her little studio before they took the last carload of their things away from the house and moved her into his apartment.

They had just gotten settled in over the following week, enjoying each other, enjoying their freedom, and finding their equilibrium after the show lifestyle, when they got a call from Harvey and Joe.

"Hey guys!" Ethan laughed when he answered his cell phone. "I didn't expect to hear from you again," he admitted to Harvey.

"Well, we just wanted to check in and see how you're both doing," Harvey told him.

"We miss you guys."

Ethan smiled at Haley and she blew him a kiss. "We're doing great."

"We also wondered if we could come by tonight to visit. The show is going to be on and we think you should watch this one," Harvey said with a smile through the phone.

Ethan sighed. "We kind of promised each other that we wouldn't watch it."

Harvey tried again. "We really think you should watch it. In fact, we want to come over and watch it with you. Make an exception for some good friends... huh? For old time's sake?" he asked hopefully.

Haley shrugged and lifted her palms in the air and Ethan nodded. "Okay. You are both more than welcome to come over. We'll see you later tonight."

She tilted her head and looked at him curiously. "Why do they want to come over here and watch the show?" she asked in confusion.

He didn't have an answer for her.

Joe and Harvey showed up and brought dinner and dessert with them, as well as good wine. "You two fed us and took such good care of us while we were filming you, that we wanted to treat tonight," Joe said with a smile.

They all got themselves ready and settled, just in time to turn on the television and watch the show.

The first scene showed Haley and Ethan arguing in the kitchen. It was footage from early on in the season. Except for the big fight at the end, they hadn't argued since the first few weeks they were living together. Not all of their footage had been used for each show. With Harvey and Joe shooting several hours a day, there was a significant amount of extra footage for use in later shows, and that became more than evident when they watched the fight between themselves.

"I can't believe they're showing such old footage. This was ages ago! Why would they do that?" Ethan asked, dumbfounded.

His answer came with the next scene. It showed him leaving the house and going to the hotel where Erica was waiting for him. There was footage of her getting ready and waiting for him seductively, and then him walking in and kissing her. Murphy had obviously gotten his way; every part of her that could legally be shown on television was being shown, and there was a lot of skin, and a lot of making out.

There were questionable moments of Ethan sucking her nipples and biting at them as he moved against her, but the camera angle and editing only showed him from the waist up at first, and because of the way he was moving, there was no way to know that his pants were on.

He saw himself pulling her hair, kissing her mouth hungrily, trailing his lips down her throat to her breasts, and the camera showed a hand squeezing and massaging her breasts, though only her nipples were barely covered as she moaned and moved with him.

Ethan frowned slightly. "That's not my hand."

The camera moved down and showed almost everything of both of them in the bed, and they were both nude, and they were unquestionably having sex with each other. The cameras showed everything that they legally could, and even used what little creative camouflage they could to add more viewable moments to the act as he rolled onto his back and she rode him hard, her breasts bouncing until he clenched at them and drew them to his mouth.

Ethan leaned all the way forward to the edge of the sofa and Haley stared in horror.

Harvey shook his head. "You didn't catch it, did you?" he asked.

Ethan shook his head. "That's not me. That is not my body! I didn't have sex with her!" he insisted adamantly.

Harvey nodded. "I know, buddy. I was there, remember? No... they got a stand-in and Erica earned that money she wanted from Murphy, and she screwed that guy's brains out. What they did, if you notice, is cut to you every now and again, but only from the waist up, and you'll see that you're only on top of her. All the scenes where she's on top, they either only show her, which seems like a natural view to someone watching, so we don't know who the bucking bronco is beneath her, or they only show him from the neck down and they focus on her body more than his.

"There... see, they are showing legs, they are showing asses and hands... her back, the guy's stomach, the sides of her breasts, her face and head, but that's where they cut the guy out... and if you watch... right.... there, see? They cut back to you really fast, using footage from before you went storming out of there. So, to anyone who doesn't know better, they would swear on a stack of bibles that you just had some seriously hot sex with Erica."

Harvey shook his head. "Bastards."

The scene shifted from the hotel to Haley crying on the phone to Leslie, telling her she didn't think she could do it and that she was going to leave him, and Haley grew irate. "That was from the first few weeks! They're using that now?" she snapped, looking in aggravation at the television.

"Oh wait," Harvey told her.

The camera then panned and showed Enrique kissing and touching Haley in the studio, but from the camera angle, no one could tell that she was drunk, and the sound was edited.

There was a voice-over from things she had said to Ethan, things about wanting him, soft sighs and moans, kissing sounds, and for all the world, it looked like she was going to sleep with Enrique. Then her jaw, and Ethan's, hit the floor when they saw Enrique on the sofa in her studio, with a woman on his lap, her back to the camera and his face visible over her shoulder, and she was rocking her body over his groin like he was an electric bull.

Enrique called out her name over and over, crying out, "Haley... oh Haley...." clinging to her breasts and sucking on her nipples, and then he came, and she came with him, and anyone watching would earnestly have believed that it was indeed Haley, screwing Enrique on the sofa in her studio.

She was thoroughly disgusted. "Oh my God! Everyone I know is going to think that's me and it isn't! How could they do that? Who the heck is that woman? What am I going to do!" She covered her mouth with her hand in horror.

Harvey frowned thoughtfully. "I think she's a hooker... or maybe a porn star. They went in and filmed it after you two moved out. All hell broke loose and they were scrambling around like their hair was on fire, trying to work out what they were going to do and who they could find in a hurry to do it. You two really left them in the lurch and I'm so glad you did. They had it coming, that's for certain."

Then the scene cut to Erica sitting at the side of their swimming pool, her legs in the water, and a skimpy suit barely covering her body. There was a man in the water who moved toward her, long blonde hair shining wet down his back, and when he reached her, she bent down and kissed him passionately.

Ethan fumed. "That's not me!" he nearly shouted at the television.

Harvey sighed. "No, it's not. They had to get the guy to get his hair wet because they couldn't replicate your hair, no matter how they tried. No wig, no dye, no model who looks like you... the closest they could do was get the stand-in's hair wet and then shoot him from the back. It looks like you, but of course, it isn't you."

Ethan slumped back against the sofa and glared hotly at the television.

Then the camera was suddenly on Murphy, who spoke from the breakfast nook of the house. He looked disappointed but calm as he carefully explained to the viewers that Haley had decided to leave Ethan for Enrique, and Ethan had succumbed to his lust for Erica, and who could blame him, Murphy said with a grin, but when Ethan was done with Erica, he had left her, and now poor Erica was on her own.

Murphy walked out to the pool and winked at the camera, nodding his head in the direction of the red headed woman sitting at the side of the pool and the man in the water.

He announced that Erica had something up her sleeve, and that the man in the pool was not Ethan. He told the viewers to tune in the following week to find out what the shows' new star Erica was up to, and who the lucky man in the pool was.

The credits began to roll and both Ethan and Haley grew loud in their vocal bashing of the charade that had been that weeks' show, but Harvey and Joe grinned at them.

"Shhh now, I know you're mad, but the show isn't over yet. Keep watching." Joe told them both. "You don't want to miss the best part. Hush now. Just watch." Joe couldn't help grinning madly, but Harvey looked like he might jump up and run right over to the television set to pounce on it.

An inset video box popped up, blocking out nearly three quarters of the screen, and it showed Ethan at the hotel with Erica, his shirt being pulled back on, his pants already on, and him telling her hell, no, that he wasn't going to sleep with her, just as it had really happened.

It was obvious that it was raw footage and hadn't been edited at all. He yelled at her, she screamed at him, her robe still on, her hair slightly tousled, but not crazy after sex ruffled, and it was obvious that nothing like the hot sex everyone had seen already, had happened between the two of them.

Then it showed him as he stormed out of the hotel room, slamming the door behind him. She screamed in fury and threw her hands in the air, wondering aloud what she was going to do about getting him to sleep with her so the producers would pay her the money they had promised her to have sex with him.

Then it showed Erica's meeting with Murphy and the video quickly pieced through her conversation about being paid to get Ethan into bed and how it hadn't happened. Then it showed Erica meeting Ethan and Haley in the hallway, and him telling Erica that he never wanted to see her again.

The camera showed him and Haley arm in arm, and him declaring that he was with the woman he loved and he wasn't ever going to be with Erica again, nor did he ever want to see her or talk to her again. It showed her storming off down the hall.

Then the camera followed Haley and Ethan into Murphy's office and it showed the entire conversation they'd had, and then the two of them walking out of the door as they left his office, and left the show. The film was digitally dated at the corner, so that there was no question of it being authentic, and filmed before all the tawdry sex scenes with the stand-ins.

The last scene was of Haley and Ethan in the kitchen at the house, talking about what had happened, exposing Murphy's illicit demands and blackmail tricks, them declaring their love for each other and saying that they were going to leave the show. Then the screen faded to black and a commercial came on.

Ethan muted the television and then turned and stared at Harvey and Joe.

"This is why you two wanted to come here and watch this tonight? You wanted to be sure that we saw the fraudulent scenes and the credits!" Ethan asked in wonder.

Harvey grinned and shrugged. "Yeah, I guess so." he answered with a smile.

Joe spoke up. "You see, we just spent so much time with you two, and we watched you fall in love for real. Then we saw what the producers were doing to you, and we just couldn't stand it, so we had a friend in the editing room who wanted to help us and help you, and we pieced it all together and came up with that. I hope it was okay for you two. We really love you guys. We want it to work out for you."

Haley looked at them both seriously. "Are you going to be fired for this?" she asked worriedly.

Harvey shrugged. "I'm sure we will, but they didn't know it was going to happen, so everyone is probably freaking out and running around with their hair on fire right now, with no idea how it happened or who did it. But when they figure it out, then yeah, we'll lose our jobs. It was still worth it, and we both talked about it, and we would both do it again, so don't you even think on it, okay?"

Haley smiled and felt tears in her eyes for them. She hugged them tight and Ethan shook their hands and then hugged them. "Thank you, guys. We would have been thrown completely under the bus on this one if it wasn't for you two saving us."

Harvey shrugged. "Well, when it's real love, you have to do what you can to keep it alive and protect it, and I was sick of working at a place like that anyway. Your lives aren't the only ones that the production team ruins on a daily basis. I think the head guy is the anti-Christ, to be honest."

Joe pulled his phone from his pocket with a little cry. "Dang thing is going crazy! Sorry... I just...." He paused and looked at it, his eyes growing wide. "Oh my God!"

Harvey looked at him in concern. "What is it? They found us out already?"

Joe shook his head and began to laugh, his finger sliding over his phone again and again, then he handed his phone to them.

"No, it's Twitter and Facebook and Snapchat... you guys are blowing up the social media sites like crazy! In fact, I think you're trending on Twitter!" He pointed to his phone and they all looked.

Sure enough, there was a huge outpouring of support for Ethan and Haley, and a tremendous shame bashing of the show, and it seemed to be growing with a viral speed.

"Oh my goodness!" Haley laughed, looking at all of the messages rolling like wildfire over Joe's phone. They read through several of them and then gave Joe his phone back, and Ethan and Haley picked up their own phones to answer the public outcry over the way the show had ended.

"Look," said Ethan. "Here's one, no, two... no... three! There are three here from the producers of the show. The first one says that they had no knowledge of the credit film and that it was a hack. The one after that says that it was a publicity stunt organized by them..." Ethan looked at Harvey incredulously.

"Now Murphy is taking credit for your hack." He shook his head and looked at it again. "This last one admits that the lovers on the show tonight were stand-ins and the producers and staff wish Haley and I much luck in our future endeavors! God! The nerve of them!"

Haley looked through the tweets on her phone and laughed again. "There's so much support here. People are saying such wonderful things!"

They read several of the messages out loud together, and all four of them responded to a handful of them, but after a while, Joe and Harvey bid the couple farewell and good luck, and asked them to keep in touch.

"We never could have gotten through this show without your intervention and help. Thank you both so much!" Haley told them, and Ethan echoed her sentiments to them.

Both men waved it off and thanked them for being such good people to work with.

Ethan looked at them both and grinned. "If you need a job reference, you put us down. We'll give you a glowing reference!"

They said goodnight and went to bed, holding one another and marveling at the way that it had all turned out.

"There is one thing I want to point out, though." Ethan said as he held her in his arms.

She looked up at him curiously. "What's that?"

"I'm a much better lover than the guy they had on that show tonight."

Haley raised one eyebrow in a sort of challenge to him. "Is that so?"

He nodded. "Yes, my dear wife, it is."

She touched her chin thoughtfully. "Well, I think I might need some convincing. You'll have to remind me again and show me just how much of a better lover you really are," she teased him, and he reached his arms around her and pulled her on top of him.

"My pleasure!" he grinned, kissing her soundly.

The night was heated with their passion and made bright with their love, and they made love once more before falling asleep in one another's arms peacefully, satisfied that things had ended well with the show and consequently, with their lives and their futures.

Epilogue

It had been two months since their final appearance on the show and the faux credits that played to a shocked nation. Ethan and Haley had found themselves the sudden darlings of the media, caught up in public adoration for the roles they had played and the true love they had found.

The public had almost no tolerance for the way the television station had handled their season. In a continual parade of interviews on television, radio, in print, and online, they shared their story, and in their new celebrity status, they were afforded several privileges, not the least of which was a hosting job for a television show for Ethan and high demand for Haley's artwork.

She had become such a successful artist overnight that she was able to open her own gallery in Los Angeles, and then she opened one in San Francisco, one in Seattle, and then one in New York. She told Ethan that if her popularity continued to grow, she would want to open some in Europe as well.

As they walked the red carpets of the spring awards shows, fans screamed their approval and adoration, and other celebrities welcomed them with open and caring arms. They were partway down the red carpet, heading into the Oscars when they were stopped for an impromptu interview.

A woman in a peach colored designer gown stopped them, waving hello and flashing her dazzling smile at them. She leaned toward them both and kissed their cheeks.

"Here we have reality television stars Ethan Richards and Haley Lawrence! How are you doing?" she asked them excitedly, as if nothing else that evening could even begin to compare to how the couple might be faring.

Ethan nodded. "We're great!" he told her happily and she grinned back at him. Then she turned her gaze to Haley. "This is a fabulous gown, you look so beautiful. Tell me, what do you two have ahead of you in the future, now that the show is behind you?

"And, before you answer that, can I just tell you that all of us were so livid at the treatment that you both endured, and we were all so relieved and glad to see how it ended, and that you both got out of it early. You found true love with each other, and there is no greater reward than that, is there? Not really!" she answered her own question and then laughed at herself lightly.

"So!" she leaned toward them. "What's coming up next for you both?"

Ethan smiled widely. "Well, I've signed two movie contracts for summer blockbuster films for next summer, and we will be filming one of those this summer and then the other this fall."

The reporter flashed him a scintillating smile. "That's fantastic! So we'll be seeing you up on the big screen instead of on our televisions! How does it feel to have such a big change happen for you like that?"

He shook his head. "It's amazing! I am ready for it, and I think it will be a good challenge, but as we all know, I love a good challenge, so this the right step for me. I'm just going to do my best and work really hard at it, and make sure that the performance I give is the best that is in me."

"That's so inspiring, like your own personal story; we can all take some hope and inspiration away from that. Great positive outlook, Ethan!"

Then she turned her attention to Haley. "Haley, what an honor to meet you, to meet you both, really, but Haley, I have to tell you, I bought two of your pieces of artwork and they are proudly displayed in my living room; side by side. I love them, they are just gorgeous."

Haley nodded and felt her cheeks warm as she smiled happily at the reporter. "Thank you!"

"You have really become one of the most popular artists in the country at this point, and I know there are lists of people waiting to get some original artwork from you. Are you finally doing what you have always wanted to do or is this newfound celebrity state a bit overwhelming for you?" the woman asked her in fascination.

Haley shrugged and nodded. "Well, it can be a little overwhelming sometimes, just from the sheer volume of people who are now connecting to me and to my life through my artwork and through Ethan's acting, but we love all of it, and we are learning so much and growing as a couple, as individuals, and as artists in our respective crafts."

Ethan squeezed her hand and smiled at her. He interrupted the reporter.

"I just want to say how proud I am of Haley's accomplishments. She works really hard on all the artwork that she does and her success is well deserved." He grinned at his wife and then leaned over and kissed her and the reporter cooed over them happily.

Then she continued her interview. "Is there anything coming up for you in the world of art, or anywhere else for that matter?" she bubbled at Haley.

Haley's eyes twinkled and she nodded. "Well, with Ethan working so hard on films this summer and fall, it kind of opens up the calendar for me, so I will be doing a nationwide gallery tour with my artwork, and I'll be in thirty cities across the country between next month and the end of the year. Most of them will be in the summer and the fall."

The reporter nodded enthusiastically. "That's wonderful! I'm sure it's going to be an enormously successful tour for you. Will you be taking the winter off? Both of you?" she asked, looking at them both in complete adoration.

Ethan nodded and smiled at Haley, giving her a little nudge. "Well, yes, and we will let you in on a secret that nobody knows. We will need the winter off, because we have just found out that we are going to be having a baby, and we will need to be home to take care of our newborn this winter, so getting all of the work done ahead of time will be a big help."

They had not announced the pregnancy to anyone except very close family and friends, and this announcement on the red carpet was the first anyone in the public had heard of it.

The reporter squealed with delight and kissed them both on the cheek again.

"Congratulations! That's about the best news that anyone could hope to find out from the two of you! True love and it just keeps on growing and getting better. Well, everyone here certainly wishes you both the best of luck, and to your new baby as well! We hope that both the films and then art shows are tremendously successful! Thank you for stopping to talk with us, and have fun tonight!"

They thanked her and walked away, heading in to the theater for the Oscar presentation event. They were stopped all along the carpet for autographs and photographs, and before they left the building for the night, Twitter was trending again, this time with their baby news, and the bulk of the messages were congratulatory and filled with love and best wishes for them.

***

Ethan's films were completed and he was happy with the work, and the production teams fully expected rave reviews. If they got them, the two films he had done would be summer blockbusters the next year, and both films would launch his acting career into the stratosphere.

Haley's art shows were all successful, so much that her work began to be put up on permanent displays in many of the cities that she visited. By the time she got back to Los Angeles at the end of fall, she had come up with the idea of beginning an art school that helped the students begin successful careers as artists anywhere in the world, and with Ethan's help, her dream was realized in a two-year period.

In time, her schools opened up in large metropolis cities across the United States, her artwork was renowned internationally, and she was able to paint, to teach, and to raise her family with much time devoted to them.

His first two movies gave him just the career boost he needed to become a hot and wanted commodity, and before the end of the next year, he had already been signed for three more movies with major companies. He was able to begin his own production company within three years, and the first thing that he and Haley did was to hire Harvey and Joe, who they had kept in close contact with over the years.

In the decades that followed, they both realized tremendous success in their work lives, they welcomed five children, two of which were twins, and their love grew stronger and deeper every day, proving the original theory of the show they had met on, that strangers put together in an arranged marriage situation can indeed fall in love; real, true, honest love. Love that lasts a lifetime.

THE END

Authors Personal Message:

Hey beautiful!

I really hope you enjoyed my novel and I would really love if you could give me a rating on the store!

Thanks in advance and if you want to check out all my other books and add them to your collection then just visit my Amazon Author page here! :)

ALSO BY CJ HOWARD

THE BILLIONAIRE'S CONVENIENT BRIDE

Billionaire Peter has found that his reputation for being a playboy is beginning to have a very negative effect on his business. So he needs a wife to help him shed his playboy image and he is willing to do what it takes to make it happen.

Emmaline is a woman with a heart of gold with big plans for her life but her job as a waitress does not make it easy for her to get where she wants to be. A payment of $3 million dollars to be the convenient bride of a billionaire for 3 years would set her up for life and it is not one she is going to turn down.

This was meant to be just a simple marriage of convenience with a clear end date and with both getting exactly what they want. However, once Peter takes time to get know Emmaline he begins to wonder if he ever wants this to end....

Made in United States
North Haven, CT
29 August 2023

40905398R00143